Treasures from
Grandma's Attic

The Grandma's Attic Series
In Grandma's Attic
More Stories from Grandma's Attic
Still More Stories from Grandma's Attic
Treasures from Grandma's Attic

Treasures from Grandma's Attic

Grandma's Attic Series
Book Four

Arleta Richardson

DAVID **C** COOK

transforming lives together

TREASURES FROM GRANDMA'S ATTIC
Published by David C Cook
4050 Lee Vance Drive
Colorado Springs, CO 80918 U.S.A.

Integrity Music Limited, a Division of David C Cook
Eastbourne, East Sussex BN23 6NT, England

The graphic circle C logo is a registered trademark of David C Cook.

LCCN 2011930765
ISBN 978-0-7814-0382-5
eISBN 978-1-4347-0457-3

The Team: Don Pape, Susan Tjaden, Amy Konyndyk,
Sarah Schultz, Jack Campbell, Karen Athen
Cover Design: Melody Christian
Illustrations: Patrice Barton

Printed in the United States of America
Third Edition 2011

12 13 14 15 16 17 18 19 20 21

122018

To the Franklins,

Bob
Ella
Christi
Ginger
Grandmother G.,

who gave me
two of life's most priceless gifts:
someone to love and someone to be loved by

Grandma's Stories

Introduction

When Grandma Was Young

More than one hundred years ago—that's when Grandma Mabel and her best friend, Sarah Jane, were girls growing up on neighboring farms in Michigan. Their lives were very different from yours. The train came through their nearby small town, but they never saw a plane or bus or taxi. The two girls couldn't call each other on the phone. They didn't have video games or dishwashers at home—they didn't even have electricity!

But in other ways, Mabel and Sarah Jane were just like you. They quarreled and made up, plotted mischief that backfired, and tried their families' patience with their dreams and schemes.

Spend a few days with these two friends. Then you decide: Are they so different from you after all?

1

Cousin Agatha

My best friend, Sarah Jane, and I were walking home from school on a cold November afternoon.

"Do you realize, Mabel, that 1886 is almost over? Another year of nothing important ever happening is nearly gone."

"Well, we still have a good bit of life ahead of us," I replied.

"You don't know that," Sarah Jane said darkly. "We're thirteen and a half. We may already have lived nearly a third of our allotted time."

"The O'Dells live to be awfully old," I told her. "So, unless I get run down by a horse and buggy, I'll probably be around awhile."

We walked along in silence. Then suddenly Sarah Jane pulled me to the side of the road. "Here's the horse and buggy that could keep you from becoming an old lady," she kidded. We turned to see my pa coming down the road.

"Want to ride the rest of the way, girls?" he called. We clambered into the buggy, and Pa clucked to Nellie.

"What did you get in town?" I asked.

"Some things for the farm and a letter for your ma." Around the next bend, Pa slowed Nellie to a halt. "Your stop, Sarah Jane."

"Thanks, Mr. O'Dell." Sarah Jane jumped down. "I'll be over to study later, Mabel. 'Bye."

"Who's the letter from?" I asked Pa.

"Can't tell from the handwriting. We'll have to wait for Ma to tell us."

When Ma opened the letter, she looked puzzled. "This is from your cousin Agatha," she said to Pa. "Why didn't she address it to you, too?"

"If I know Aggie, she wants something," Pa declared. "And she figured you'd be more likely to listen to her sad story."

Ma read the letter and shook her head at Pa. "She just wants to come for Thanksgiving. Now aren't you ashamed of talking that way?"

"No, I'm not. That's what Aggie *says* she wants. You can be sure there's more there than meets the eye. Are you going to tell her to come ahead?"

"Why, of course!" Ma exclaimed. "If I were a widowed lady up in years, I'd want to be with family on Thanksgiving. Why shouldn't I tell her to come?"

Pa took his hat from the peg by the door and started for the barn, where my older brothers, Reuben and Roy, were already at work. "Don't say I didn't warn you," he remarked as he left.

"What did Pa warn you about?" I asked as soon as the door closed behind him. "What does Cousin Agatha want?"

"I don't believe Pa was talking to you," Ma replied. "You heard me say that she wants to come for Thanksgiving."

"Yes, but Pa said—"

"That's enough, Mabel. We won't discuss it further."

I watched silently as Ma sat down at the kitchen table and answered Cousin Agatha's letter.

Snow began to fall two days before the holiday, and Pa had to hitch up the sleigh to go into town and meet the train. "It will be just our misfortune to have a real blizzard and be snowed in with that woman for a week," he grumbled.

"Having Aggie here a few days won't hurt you," Ma said. "The way you carry on, you'd think she was coming to stay forever!"

Pa's look said he considered that a distinct possibility. As I helped Ma with the pies, I questioned her about Cousin Agatha.

"Has she been here before? I can't remember seeing her."

"I guess you were pretty small last time Agatha visited," Ma replied. "I expect she gets lonely in that big house in the city."

"What do you suppose she wants besides dinner?" I ventured.

"Friendly company," Ma snapped. "And we're going to give it to her."

When the pies were in the oven, I hung around the window, watching for the sleigh. It was nearly dark when I heard the bells on Nellie's harness ring out across the snow.

"They're coming, Ma," I called. Ma hurried to the door with the lamp held high over her head. The boys and I crowded behind her. Pa jumped down from the sleigh and turned to help Cousin Agatha.

"I don't need any assistance from you, James," a firm voice spoke. "I'm perfectly capable of leaving any conveyance under my own power."

"She talks like a book!" Roy whispered, and Reuben poked him. I watched in awe as a tall, unbending figure sailed into the kitchen.

"Well, Maryanne," she said, "it's good to see you." She removed her big hat, jabbed a long hat pin into it, and handed the hat to me. "You must be Mabel."

I nodded wordlessly.

"What's the matter? Can't you speak?" she boomed.

"Yes, ma'am." I gulped nervously.

"Then don't stand there bobbing your head like a monkey on a stick. People will think you have no sense. You can put that hat in my room."

I stared openmouthed at this unusual person until a gentle push from Ma sent me in the direction of the guest room.

After dinner and prayers, Pa rose with the intention of going to the barn.

"James!" Cousin Agatha's voice stopped him. "Surely you aren't going to do the chores by yourself with these two great hulking fellows sitting here, are you?"

The two great hulking fellows leaped for the door with a speed I didn't know they had.

"I should guess so," Cousin Agatha exclaimed with satisfaction. "If there's anything I can't abide, it's a lazy child."

As she spoke, Cousin Agatha pulled Ma's rocker to the stove and lowered herself into it. "This chair would be more comfortable if there were something to put my feet on," she said, "but I suppose one can't expect the amenities in a place like this."

I looked at Ma for some clue as to what *amenities* might mean. This was not a word we had encountered in our speller.

"Run into the parlor and get the footstool, Mabel," Ma directed.

After Cousin Agatha was settled with her hands in her lap and her feet off the cold floor, I started the dishes.

"Maryanne, don't you think Mabel's dress is a mite too short?"

Startled, I looked down at my dress.

"No," Ma's calm voice replied. "She's only thirteen, you know. I don't want her to be grown up too soon."

"There is such a thing as modesty, you know." Cousin Agatha sniffed.

Pa and the boys returned just then, so Ma didn't

answer. I steered an uneasy path around Cousin Agatha all evening. For the first time I could remember, I was glad when bedtime came.

The next day was Thanksgiving, and the house was filled with the aroma of good things to eat. From her rocker, Cousin Agatha offered suggestions as Ma scurried about the kitchen.

"Isn't it time to baste the turkey, Maryanne? I don't care for dry fowl.

"I see the boys running around out there with that mangy dog as though they had nothing to do. Shouldn't they be chopping wood or something?

"I should think Mabel could be helping you instead of reading a book. If there's one thing I can't abide—"

"Mabel will set the table when it's time," Ma put in. "Maybe you'd like to peel some potatoes?"

The horrified look on Cousin Agatha's face said she wouldn't consider it, so Ma withdrew her offer.

A bump on the door indicated that the "mangy dog" was tired of the cold. I laid down my book and let Pep in. He made straight for the stove and his rug.

"Mercy!" Cousin Agatha cried. "Do you let that—that animal in the kitchen?"

"Yes," Ma replied. "He's not a young dog any longer. He isn't any bother, and he does enjoy the heat."

"Humph." Agatha pulled her skirts around her. "I wouldn't allow any livestock in my kitchen. Can't think what earthly good a dog can be." She glared at Pep, who responded with a thump of his tail and a sigh of contentment.

"Dumb creature," Cousin Agatha muttered.

"Pep isn't dumb, Cousin Agatha," I said. "He's really the smartest dog I know."

"I was not referring to his intellect or lack of it," she told me. "*Dumb* indicates an inability to speak. You will have to concede that he is unable to carry on a conversation."

I was ready to dispute that, too, but Ma shook her head. Cousin Agatha continued to give Pep disparaging glances.

"Didn't you ever have any pets at your house, Cousin Agatha?" I asked.

"Pets? I should say not! Where in the Bible does it say that God made animals for man's playthings? They're meant to earn their keep, not sprawl out around the house absorbing heat."

"Oh, Pep works," I assured her. "He's been taking the cows out and bringing them back for years now."

Cousin Agatha was not impressed. She sat back in the rocker and eyed Pep with disfavor. "The one thing I can't abide, next to a lazy child, is a useless animal—and in the house!"

I began to look nervously at Ma, thinking she might send Pep to the barn to keep the peace. But she went on about her work, serenely ignoring Cousin Agatha's hints. I was glad when it was time to set the table.

After we had eaten, Pa took the Bible down from the cupboard and read our Thanksgiving chapter, Psalm 100. Then he prayed, thanking the Lord for Cousin Agatha and asking the Lord's blessing on her just as he did on the rest of us. When he had finished, Cousin Agatha spoke up.

"I believe that I will stay here until Christmas, James. Then, if I find it to my liking, I could sell the house in the city and continue on with you. Maryanne could use some help in teaching these children how to be useful."

In the stunned silence that followed, I looked at Pa and Ma to see how this news had affected them. Ma looked pale. Before Pa could open his mouth to answer, Cousin Agatha rose from the table. "I'll just go to my room for a bit of rest," she said. "We'll discuss this later."

When she had left, we gazed at each other helplessly.

"Is there anything in the Bible that tells you what to do now?" I asked Pa.

"Well, it says if we don't love our brother whom we can see, how can we love God whom we can't see? I think that probably applies to cousins as well."

"I'd love her better if I couldn't see her," Reuben declared. "We don't have to let her stay, do we, Pa?"

"No, we don't have to," Pa replied. "We could ask her to leave tomorrow as planned. But I'm not sure that would be right. What do you think, Ma?"

"I wouldn't want to live alone in the city," Ma said slowly. "I can see that she would prefer the company of a family. I suppose we should ask her to stay until Christmas."

"I think she already asked herself," Roy ventured. "But she did say *if* she found things to her liking …"

We all looked at Roy. Pa said, "You're not planning something that wouldn't be to her liking, are you?"

"Oh, no, sir!" Roy quickly answered. "Not me."

Pa sighed. "I'm not sure I'd blame you. She's not an easy person to live with. We'll all have to be especially patient with her."

There wasn't much Thanksgiving atmosphere in the kitchen as we did the dishes.

"How can we possibly stand it for another whole month?" I moaned.

"The Lord only sends us one day at a time," Ma informed me. "Don't worry about more than that. When the other days arrive, you'll probably find out you worried about all the wrong things."

As soon as the work was finished, I put on my coat and walked over to Sarah Jane's.

"What will you do if she stays on after Christmas?" Sarah Jane asked.

"I'll just die."

"I thought you were going to be a long-living O'Dell."

"I changed my mind," I retorted. "What would you do if you were in my place?"

"I'd probably make her life miserable so she'd want to leave."

"You know I couldn't get away with that. Pa believes that Christian love is the best solution."

"All right, then," Sarah Jane said with a shrug. "Love her to death."

As though to fulfill Pa's prediction, snow began to fall heavily that night. By morning we were snowed in.

"Snowed in?" Cousin Agatha repeated. "You mean unable to leave the house at all?"

"That's right," Pa replied. "This one is coming straight down from Canada."

Cousin Agatha looked troubled. "I don't like this. I don't like it at all."

"We'll be all right," Ma reassured her. "We have plenty of wood and all the food we need."

But Cousin Agatha was not to be reassured. I watched her stare into the fire and twist her handkerchief around her fingers. *Why, she's frightened!* I thought. This old lady had been directing things all her life, and here was something she couldn't control. Suddenly I felt sorry for her.

"Cousin Agatha," I said, "we have fun when we're snowed in. We play games and pop corn and tell stories. You'll enjoy it. I know you will!"

I ran over and put my arms around her shoulders and kissed her on the cheek. She looked at me in surprise.

"That's the first time anyone has hugged me since I can remember," she said. "Do you really like me, Mabel?"

Right then I knew that I did like Cousin Agatha a whole lot. Behind her stern front was another person who needed to be loved and wanted.

"Oh, yes, Cousin Agatha," I replied. "I really do. You'll see what a good time we'll have together."

The smile that lit her face was bright enough to chase away any gloom that had settled over the kitchen. And deep down inside, I felt real good.

2

A New Friend

Sarah Jane and I were approaching the school yard one morning, talking about nothing in particular, when we both came to a dead stop. Straight ahead stood a new girl leaning against a tree, watching the other children play.

"Who do you think that is?" Sarah Jane asked. "I didn't know anyone new had moved in."

"I don't know," I said, "but she has the reddest hair I've ever seen. Do you suppose she has a temper to match?"

"I hope not," Sarah Jane replied. "I wouldn't want that much mad directed at me."

We walked over to greet her. "I'm Mabel," I said. "What's your name?"

"Mary Etta Rose Amanda Morgan."

Sarah Jane's mouth dropped open. "Four given names? Do you use all of them?"

"Just Mary. My mother didn't want to disappoint any of her sisters, so she named me after all of them! I hope we're going to be friends," she continued. "I don't know anyone here."

Our teacher, Miss Gibson, came out just then to ring the bell, and we all filed into the schoolhouse. Mary was welcomed and settled into a seat behind Sarah Jane and me. During study time, I felt a poke in my back.

"Who's that good-looking boy by the second window?" Mary whispered.

I looked to see who she meant. "That's my brother Roy," I whispered back.

"Your brother?" Mary squeaked, and Miss Gibson looked disapprovingly in our direction. No more was said until recess time. Then Mary took hold of my arm and drew me to the side of the school.

"I think we should be best friends, don't you?" she said. "We can have secrets from all the others."

"I've never had a secret from Sarah Jane," I blurted. "What would we want to keep from her?"

"For goodness' sake, Mabel!" Mary exclaimed. "Maybe it's time you got away from her. I could tell right away that Sarah Jane isn't as mature and interesting as you are. There are lots of things we could talk about that she wouldn't even understand."

This was a new idea to me, and I stared at Mary in fascination. Was I really mature and interesting?

"By the way," Mary went on, "how old is your brother?"

"He's almost fifteen," I replied. "Why?"

"I just wondered," she said with a shrug. "Does he have a girlfriend?"

"A girlfriend! Roy? He thinks the only thing girls are good for is to tease."

"Don't worry," Mary said. "He'll change his mind. Come on, let's get a drink of water."

She sauntered toward the well, and I tagged along after her. If she wanted the boys to notice her, she wasn't disappointed.

"They couldn't help but see her," Sarah Jane said to me on the way home. "Her hair stands out like a fire in a wood box. You'd better watch out, Mabel, or you'll get into trouble."

I stopped in my tracks and stared at her. "Me! What have I done to be in trouble?"

"Nothing yet, I guess. But if you're around Mary Etta Rose Amanda Morgan very much, she'll see to it that you do something."

"That's ridiculous!" I exclaimed. "All she said was that she wanted to be friends."

"And?" Sarah Jane prodded.

"She asked how old Roy was and if he had a girlfriend," I finished lamely.

"Aha!" Sarah Jane cried. "See there? She's trying to use you to get to your brother!"

"Nobody uses me for anything!" I shouted at her. "I think you're just jealous!"

I stomped away from Sarah Jane with my nose in the air. Then I turned and went back. "Why are we fighting over someone we don't even know?" I asked her. "Do you really think Mary would try to do that?"

Sarah Jane nodded. "I'm sure of it, Mabel. Something tells me that she's not up to any good. I just feel it in my bones."

In the days that followed, Mary continued to single me out for special favors. She brought candy and chocolate cake for lunchtime. She loaned me a book to take home. I was flattered, but I made sure we spent lunch and recess with all the other girls.

One Friday, about a month after Mary had arrived, Sarah Jane was sick, and I walked to school alone. Mary walked out to meet me. "Come here, Mabel. I have something to show you."

I followed her to the corner of the school yard. "What is it?" I asked. "Is it a secret?"

Mary nodded and pulled a small box out of her dress pocket. "Look," she whispered. She opened the box, and there lay the most beautiful ring I had ever seen.

"Ooh! Where did you get it?"

"Someone gave it to me," she replied. "Do you like it? Here, try it on."

I put the ring on my finger.

"You can have it if you'll do something for me," Mary said.

"Have it! You mean to keep?"

She nodded. "Do you want it?"

"What do you want me to do?"

Mary looked around to be sure no one could hear. "I want you to get Roy to come over to my house."

"How would I ever do that?" I exclaimed. "He's never done anything I asked him to in his life."

Mary thought a moment. "Tell him my aunt Rose wants him to do some work for her."

"Does she?"

"No, but that doesn't make any difference. He won't find that out until he gets there. By then it will be too late."

I opened my mouth to say it would be dishonest, but just then the bell rang. We hurried into the schoolroom, where I had a hard time concentrating on my lessons. Visions of the beautiful ring kept getting in the way.

What if I were to tell Roy that Mary said her aunt wanted him to do some work for her? That wouldn't be a lie, would it? No, but it would be deceitful. Was the ring worth it?

At recess, Mary pulled me away from the others again. "Are you going to do it?" she asked.

I shook my head. "No. I can't tell Roy something that isn't true."

"He wouldn't know it wasn't true," she persisted.

"Maybe not," I replied, "but I would. I just couldn't do it."

"I thought you were different from these other kids," Mary said in disgust. "But you're as dumb as they are. You'll be sorry!" She turned and walked away, and I followed her slowly back to the schoolhouse.

On the way home I stopped by to tell Sarah Jane about it. "So it looks as though I lost a friend and a ring," I concluded.

"I didn't see the ring," Sarah Jane declared, "but you haven't lost much of a friend. I wonder why she said you'd be sorry."

"I don't know," I replied. "Maybe she'll give it to some-one else with a brother! The worst thing she can do is refuse to talk to me anymore. And I'm not sure that would be bad."

But that wasn't the worst thing Mary could do. On Monday morning Ma called to me as I started out for school.

"Will you take this recipe to Miss Gibson? She asked me about it at church yesterday. Here, I'll put it in your sweater pocket."

As Ma tucked the paper in my pocket, she felt something hard in the corner. "What's this?" she asked, and drew it out.

I stared in astonishment. "That's Mary's ring. I don't know how it got there," I told Ma. "I didn't take it."

"Of course you didn't," Ma said. "But it didn't just jump into your pocket, either. You'd better get it back to Mary as soon as possible."

Sarah Jane and I talked it over on the way to school. "I think I'll just put it on her desk and not say anything about it," I decided.

"I wouldn't," Sarah Jane declared. "I'd let everyone know she tried to make me look guilty. She shouldn't get away with that."

"Maybe she didn't put it there," I suggested. "Maybe someone else took it and—"

"Oh, Mabel! You know that isn't the way it happened. She threatened to get even with you, didn't she? So this is the way to do it."

We got to school just as the bell rang, and I had no chance to speak to Mary. As soon as school was opened, she raised her hand. "Miss Gibson, someone took my ring."

"Oh, I don't think so, Mary," Miss Gibson replied. "You must have just mislaid it. Have you looked through your desk?"

Mary shook her head. "No, ma'am. I didn't mislay it. I know who took it, because I saw it on her finger. It was Mabel O'Dell."

In the silence that followed, I could feel my face getting red. If Mary had wanted to make me look guilty, she had succeeded. My mouth opened, but not a word came out.

"Is this true, Mabel?" Miss Gibson asked me. "Do you have Mary's ring?"

"No, er, yes, ma'am. That is, I have the ring, but I didn't take it."

"That's a likely story," Mary snorted. "How would you get it if you didn't take it?"

"Where is the ring now, Mabel? Would you bring it to me, please?" Miss Gibson held out her hand, and I walked to the front of the room and handed it to her.

"Where did you get it?" she asked me.

"I found it in my pocket," I said. "I just discovered it this morning."

"And you didn't put it there?"

I shook my head. "No, ma'am."

"Someone had to put it in your pocket," Mary accused. "If you didn't, who did?" She looked triumphantly at Miss Gibson.

"That's a question, all right," Miss Gibson said. "We'll have to find out who it was."

"Her," said a little voice from the front row. "I saw her do it." Belinda was pointing at Mary.

Miss Gibson looked confused, and Mary was angry. "Are you going to believe that little infant?" she sputtered.

"Belinda, are you sure?" Miss Gibson asked her. "When did you see this happen?"

"On Friday," Belinda said. "Right after school. She put the ring in Mabel's pocket and then she ran outside. I saw her."

Miss Gibson looked at me and then back at Mary. "I'll keep the ring, and we'll talk about this at recess. Open your books, please, and begin to study at once."

I returned to my seat and opened my book, but I didn't see much that was in it. What if Miss Gibson didn't believe Belinda? How could I prove that I hadn't taken the ring? It was a long wait until recess.

As soon as the others had left, Miss Gibson turned to Mary. "Why did you want us to think Mabel had stolen your ring?" she asked her. "Do you realize what a serious accusation this is?"

"But she did …," Mary began. Then, as Miss Gibson looked at her steadily, Mary began to cry. "I thought Mabel would be my friend, but she wouldn't do what I wanted her to."

"Is someone a friend only when she does as you say?" Miss Gibson asked gently. "I think you have the wrong idea about friendship. Perhaps you can ask Mabel to forgive you and start over again."

Mary glanced at me sullenly. "Sorry," she muttered.

"That was the sorriest sorry I ever heard," I told Sarah Jane later. "But I don't think she'll try something like that again. And your bones were right—you felt trouble, and it came."

"They're very seldom wrong," Sarah Jane replied smugly. "The sooner you learn to trust them, the happier you'll be!"

We laughed and headed for home together.

3

Christmas Spirit

I shook the snow off the holly berries and sniffed the cold air appreciatively. "Aren't you glad you don't live where it's always cold or always hot?" I asked Ma.

"I suppose you could get used to anything," Ma replied. "But, yes, I'm always happy with a change of seasons. It wouldn't seem like Christmas to me without snow."

"I believe Christmas is here when the schoolhouse is decorated and the program ready," I said. "It's going to be so pretty this year. We're going out today to cut greens and find a tree. This holly would look nice too. Wouldn't it?"

Ma agreed that it would. "Mabel, take the milk to the house, and I'll cut some holly for you," she offered.

I had taken the milk pail and started up the lane, when something occurred to me. "I don't ever remember you handing me the milk pail without warning me not to spill it," I said. "Does that mean you think I'm a more dependable age now?"

"It means you're at an age where you can clean up after yourself." Ma laughed. "You learn to be careful in a hurry when you have to mop the floor and wash your own clothes."

The morning at school dragged. Steam rose from the wet mittens arranged around the hot stove, and everyone who passed a frosted window had to put a wet finger on it to trace the pattern of the ice.

"Isn't it almost noon?" Wesley asked. "I have too much Christmas spirit to pay attention to schoolwork."

"Oh!" said Miss Gibson. "Just what is 'Christmas spirit,' anyway?"

"Peace-on-earth-goodwill-to-men," Sarah Jane answered glibly. "With maybe a little fun thrown in just for … the fun of it!"

"I understand your impatience," Miss Gibson admitted. "This is a special time of year, and it is fun. But I hope we can learn something about the true meaning of Christmas too. Let's stop and eat now, and then we'll go look for a tree."

Everyone was in favor of that, and we ran to collect and open our lunch pails.

"Oh, dear," cried Belinda. "My sandwich is frozen!"

"We can fix that," Miss Gibson told her. "Unwrap your sandwich and lay it on the lid of your dinner pail, then we'll put that on the coal shovel and stick it in the stove. It will soon be toasty and warm."

That worked so well that the rest of us wanted to try it. "Mmm. Hot corn bread," Warren said. "This is almost as good as being home."

"And doesn't it smell just like a kitchen?" I put in. "There are a lot of things that cook on the stove all day. Why couldn't we have a hot dinner right here?"

"Soup is good," Sarah Jane chimed in. "It could simmer away while we work."

"That sounds delightful," Miss Gibson agreed. "But how much work would we get done between sniffs?"

"Not much," we admitted, laughing. "It's hard enough now to wait for noontime."

Everyone finished eating in record time, and we were soon bundled up and ready to go. The woods behind the school always produced the most beautiful branches and a tree that was just the right size. Each class made decorations and tried to keep them a secret until the day came to hang them on the tree. Sarah Jane and I were the only eighth graders, and since Wesley was alone in the seventh grade, Miss Gibson suggested that he join us.

"I can see his contribution right now," Sarah Jane confided. "An apple with a bite out of it. Or a gingerbread man with a leg missing."

"You're probably right," I agreed. "He does love to eat. Maybe we can get him to carve a wooden cookie and paint it."

The woods were sheltered and didn't seem quite as cold. When we had gathered all the branches we could carry, we trudged back to the schoolhouse.

"We'll leave the tree and greens outside," Miss Gibson decided. "They'd dry out pretty fast in the warm room. Let's start working on the ornaments, shall we?"

Just before dismissal time, we drew names for presents. Each year Miss Gibson would put all our names in a box, and we would each bring a Christmas gift for the person whose name we drew. We weren't allowed to put a name back unless we picked our own.

"I hope I don't get your name," I said to Sarah Jane. "And I'd rather not have Warren Carter's, either."

"It's nice to be included in such intelligent company," she replied, "but I'm not exactly flattered."

"Oh, you know what I mean. I give you a present anyway. I don't want you to get mine, either."

"I know." Sarah Jane nodded. "I was kidding."

On the way home Sarah Jane said, "Well, my present isn't going to be hard to fix. A big box of candy will do nicely."

"Wesley?" I guessed.

"Right. I'll make some chocolate fudge and some divinity. Whose name did you get?"

"Hannah's. I'd like to think of something to give her that would make her smile."

"You'll never do it," Sarah Jane said emphatically. "She has absolutely no Christmas spirit. Just hope she didn't get your name. I heard her say she wouldn't bring a gift if she didn't get a name she wanted."

"Want to trade with me?"

"No, thank you. At least Wesley can be depended upon to like what he gets, provided it stands still long enough for him to eat it."

"Do you think we ought to tell Miss Gibson about Hannah?" I asked. "We don't want the party to be ruined."

"I don't think Hannah would really do what she said," Sarah Jane replied. "She likes to complain, but she's not mean."

"I suppose you're right. Anyway, this is too nice a day to worry about it."

"There's a whole week of school until Christmas vacation," I said to Ma as we got supper. "I wonder if I can wait that long."

"I think it's possible," Ma replied. "Do you want to know how to make the time seem to go faster?"

"Oh, yes! How can I do that?"

"Plan to get more things done than you have time to finish," Ma said. "I know that works, because I've been doing it for years."

"I have plenty to work on," I said. "I have to finish Sarah Jane's gift and make something for Hannah, not to mention make Christmas presents for the family and get ready for the Christmas program."

"You won't have a problem waiting." Ma laughed. "That's already enough activity for two weeks."

Miss Gibson allowed us time to work on Christmas projects and overlooked the extra noise and restlessness. The decorations for the tree were better than they had ever been. Even the first graders' strings of cranberries and pop-corn were longer and prettier.

"Wesley," Sarah Jane inquired one afternoon, "where are the rest of the candy canes for the tree?"

"I guess I ate a few," he confessed.

"A few! There are only two here, and we started out with ten! Now what do we do?"

"I'll get Ma to make some cookies to hang up," Wesley promised. "I'll bring them in the morning."

"If I believed that, I'd believe anything," Sarah Jane muttered. "You could eat a dozen cookies between your house and the road. I'll stop by and get them myself to be sure they get here."

"Honestly, Wesley," I said, "by the time you're ready to graduate, they'll have to roll you out of the schoolhouse."

Wesley grinned. "What would a growing boy be without an appetite?"

"I don't know," I replied. "I've never seen one."

The week did pass swiftly, as Ma had predicted. With her help, I had made a pretty Christmas apron for Hannah. It was wrapped in green tissue paper and tied with red ribbon. The program was ready too.

"The older pupils are putting on a play instead of

reciting pieces," I told the family. "It's a Christmas story, but I can't tell you about it because it's a surprise."

"What are you, Santa Claus or one of the reindeer?" Reuben teased.

"That is not funny," I replied stiffly. "There is more to Christmas than Santa Claus. There's also a spirit of kindness and giving."

"Kindness we can use a lot more of," Pa remarked, looking at Reuben. "Suppose we show a little to the animals and bed them down for the night. Shall we, boys?"

"I'll be home at noon tomorrow," I told Ma as we did the dishes. "We have to be back early tomorrow evening to get everything ready for the program."

"I'm sure it will be just fine," Ma said. "I'm looking forward to it."

The program went off with hardly a mistake, and the time soon arrived for distributing the gifts. Wesley was chosen to hand them out as the names were called.

"He was born for the job," Sarah Jane whispered to me. "All he lacks is the beard and red suit."

One by one the gaily wrapped presents were brought to their owners, who shook them and poked them to try to guess what might be inside.

"Mabel, yours must be at the bottom," Sarah Jane said.

"Either that or Hannah got my name," I joked.

Finally there was just one gift left. The name on it was David Ross. He was sick and hadn't come to the program.

"You didn't get one!" Sarah Jane said in disbelief. "I didn't think she really meant it."

"And I gave her that pretty apron," I said. "See if I ever do anything nice for her again!"

The rest of the evening didn't seem quite so exciting to me, and I was glad when it was time to go home.

"It's not just that I didn't get a present," I explained to Ma on the way home. "The worst part is that she embarrassed me in front of my friends! It just isn't fair. I wish I hadn't given her that apron."

"Do you give a gift just to get one in return?" Ma asked me quietly. "Is that what the spirit of kindness and giving is all about?"

"No, I guess it isn't," I answered. I was ashamed of myself for feeling as I did, but I was disappointed. It was hard to forgive Hannah for what she had done.

On Sunday I had a cold and stayed home from church. When the family returned, Pa came over to the couch where I lay and dropped a box wrapped in tissue paper beside me.

"This is yours," he said. "It's from David Ross. He had your name, but since he couldn't get to the program, his folks brought his gift to church today."

Hannah hadn't gotten my name! I had wrongly accused her and been resentful about something that hadn't even happened.

"I was so sure I knew all about the Christmas spirit," I told Sarah Jane when I saw her. "I feel awful for thinking such mean things about Hannah."

"You should," Sarah Jane replied. "After all, you know it's more blessed to give than to receive. And since you can use all the blessing you can get, you'd better be sure to give me a Christmas present!"

4

The Perfect Paper

"Why aren't you eating your breakfast, Mabel?" Ma asked me. "Don't you feel well?"

"I'm fine, Ma," I replied. "Just nervous, I guess. We have a big arithmetic test today, and I'm afraid I'll make foolish mistakes. I know how to do the problems, but it seems as though I always slip up somewhere. I just never notice until after the papers are graded."

"Try not to be anxious about it," Ma said. "Remember, 'in everything by prayer and supplication with thanksgiving let your requests be made known unto God. And the peace of God shall keep your heart and mind through Christ Jesus.' That's in the fourth chapter of Philippians. We'll pray about it, and I'm sure you'll do just fine."

"Thanks, Ma. I'll be especially careful, too. Just once I'd like to get ahead of Warren Carter. He thinks he's so smart in arithmetic that no one can beat him."

"I hope that's not the only reason you want a good grade," Ma said. "That's hardly a worthy motive."

"Oh, no," I assured her. "That's not the only reason." *But it's the main one,* I admitted to myself. "If I could just show Warren that a girl can do as well as he can, I'd be happy."

On the way to school I told Sarah Jane, "I'm not going to make a single mistake on the test."

"How can you be so sure?" she wanted to know. "Have you seen the answers?"

"Of course not. I haven't even seen the problems. I just know. We prayed about it this morning. I can't wait to see Warren's face when I get a hundred percent."

"Maybe the Lord will let you make a mistake to take you down a peg," Sarah Jane suggested. "You'd be too proud if you got a perfect paper."

"Thanks a lot," I retorted. "I thought you were on my side."

"Oh, I am," Sarah Jane said. "I'm just reminding you that pride goes before a fall."

"I don't know what I'd do without you," I declared. "If my conscience ever wears out, I'll always have you."

Sarah Jane smiled. "What are friends for? I just wish I had a chance to get a hundred on that test. I know I'll make mistakes."

The test was every bit as hard as I thought it would be. I worked slowly and carefully, and when Miss Gibson said we had just enough time to check our work, I went back over each problem. I was satisfied that I had made no errors when I turned in the paper.

"I'm glad that's over," Sarah Jane said as we ate lunch. "I'll be happy with a passing grade."

"Did you ask the Lord to help you?" I questioned her.

"You can't ask the Lord to make you smarter than you are," a voice said. We turned to find Warren Carter standing behind us. "Anyway, I don't think God pays attention to things like schoolwork. He has more important matters to take care of."

"There may be a few things you don't know," I told him. "Who do you think gave you your brains, anyway?"

"God did. And He expects me to use them, not come asking Him to pass a test for me. But I suppose girls need all the help they can get." Warren walked away, leaving us to glare after him.

"Someday he's going to fail something," I predicted. "He'll see how important it is to pray."

"The wicked do prosper," Sarah Jane said with a sigh. "He probably did as well on the test as you did, without praying about it. That will make him all the more unbearable. You should have thought to pray that he'd make a mistake."

"Well, I did pray that I'd get a better grade than his," I admitted. "I certainly studied hard enough to deserve it. He thinks he knows it all so well that he doesn't have to work. He's the one who needs to be taken down a peg."

Sarah Jane nodded in agreement, and we went back to the room for afternoon classes.

When I got home after school, Ma was waiting for me with fresh cookies and milk. "How did it go?" she asked. "Do you think you did a good job?"

"It was hard," I replied, "but I did my very best."

"That's all we expect of you," Ma said. "No one needs to do better than that."

"Ma, do you think God made boys smarter than girls?"

"No, I don't. I'm sure there are some boys who are more intelligent than some girls, but it works the other way around too. I don't think God favors boys over girls."

"Warren Carter does. And he says you might as well not pray about a test, because God isn't interested in that kind of thing."

"That's too bad," Ma said. "I find it a comfort to believe that God cares about anything that affects His children. There's nothing too small to pray about."

I waited impatiently for Sarah Jane to reach our gate the next morning. "Can't you hurry a little?" I called. "What took you so long?"

"I had to change my dress," she replied. "Besides, I didn't know school was a place you hurried to. What's the rush?"

"I want to see the grade on my paper."

"Not I," she stated firmly. "That's a pleasure I'd put off indefinitely if I could. I hope it won't ruin your day if you don't get a hundred."

The opening exercises seemed to take a lot longer than usual. I was almost chewing my fingernails before Miss Gibson picked up the test papers from her desk.

"The examination was especially hard this time," Miss Gibson announced. "There was only one paper with a hundred percent, and that was Mabel O'Dell's. Warren Carter had ninety-eight."

I felt the blood rush to my face, and Sarah Jane's mouth dropped open. "You did it!" she exclaimed. "You beat Warren by two points!"

"I'm proud of you, Mabel." Miss Gibson smiled at me as I went to get my paper. "You worked hard on this. And you, too, Warren," she said to him. "One error is still an excellent test."

But not perfect, I thought triumphantly. It would have done my heart good to say it out loud, but I knew it was better not to. Warren's look of disbelief was reward enough for me.

"I'll have to admit I didn't think you could do it," Sarah Jane said. "Or maybe I thought Warren couldn't make a mistake. I'm sure proud of you. Your folks will be too."

I knew they would be pleased, and I put my paper in my books to take home. It was hard to concentrate on English and history and science the rest of the day. I noticed Warren wasn't doing very well either, but I didn't feel sorry for him. He deserved it for what he said about God and girls.

I showed Ma the test as soon as I got home and then put it on the table for Pa to see when he came in. "I don't know when I've enjoyed anything as much as beating

Warren Carter," I said to Ma. "Maybe he won't be so sure of everything from now on."

"Don't gloat," Ma said. "Think how it would be if you were in his place."

I tried to do that, but it was hard not to believe he had it coming. After supper I helped Ma with the dishes. Then I spread my homework out on the table while Pa was looking over my test paper.

"Mabel," he said, "this answer isn't right."

I dropped my book and hurried over to him. "It has to be, Pa! Miss Gibson corrects them from the key in her book!"

"Books have been known to be wrong," Pa replied. "I've worked this out twice and got the same answer both times. You look at my figures."

I carefully checked the problem that Pa had done. There was no doubt; mine was wrong.

"How could that book have an error in it?" I cried. "People depend on books to be correct. Miss Gibson didn't see it!"

"She wasn't expecting it," Pa said. "I'm sure she didn't think it was necessary to work every problem when she had the key."

"How did you find it? With all the problems on that test, how did you see the wrong one?"

"Just by chance, I guess," Pa answered. "I thought I'd see if I still remembered how to do these and I just picked one to work."

"Oh, this is awful!" I moaned.

"There's nothing so awful about one mistake," Pa said. "You still have an excellent test paper."

"But not perfect," I replied. "I don't want just excellent— I want perfect. I'll die. I feel sick just thinking about it."

"It hardly seems sensible to quit school over one arithmetic problem," Ma pointed out. "Just think of the favor you'll be doing the people who got it right."

"I am thinking," I said. "What if that's the one Warren missed? He'll have the hundred and I'll have ninety-eight. He'll never let me forget it. In fact, he'll claim he was right about not praying. It wasn't any use."

Ma was silent while I gathered up my books to go to my room. "I'm sorry, Mabel. I know how disappointed you are. It's especially hard to think you have a perfect paper and then have it taken away from you."

I nodded. "Warren was right about one thing, though. He said I couldn't ask God to take a test for me—especially not when I wanted to prove that I was better than someone else."

I debated about whether to tell Sarah Jane on the way to school. Finally I decided she might as well know sooner as later.

"I'm not going to tell anyone else but Miss Gibson," I said. "She can tell the others."

"Why tell her?" Sarah Jane wanted to know. "The mistake in the book wasn't your fault."

"The mistake on my paper was," I replied. "It would be cheating to just let it go."

"How about putting down a wrong answer on your next test?" she suggested. "Then you'd be even."

I shook my head. "I couldn't do that. It wouldn't be fair to the ones who had it right."

"I was just trying to think of some way to keep Warren Carter from crowing about how great boys are," Sarah Jane said with a shrug. "I didn't think you'd go along with it."

Miss Gibson was surprised when I told her what Pa had found. "I believe that's the one Warren had marked wrong!" she exclaimed.

"I was pretty sure it would be." I sighed. "Justice

wouldn't be served if it weren't. I got what was coming to me for thinking I was so much smarter than he is."

"Mabel," Miss Gibson said, "I'd rather have an honest student with errors in her work than a dishonest one with a perfect record. When you are grown, people will be more interested in your integrity than in your knowledge of arithmetic."

That pleased me, but the real surprise came at lunchtime when Warren sidled over to where we were sitting. "That was a brave thing to do, Mabel," he said. "I don't think I'd have wanted to. You might even have the right idea about praying. You're really all right—for a girl."

5

Wesley's Lesson

"Sarah Jane! Look out!" Too late. She was sprawled on her face, her books and dinner pail in a wide circle around her.

"Are you all right?" I knelt down beside her and rolled her over on her back. "Is anything broken?"

"It will be if you keep pushing me around," she protested. Slowly she opened her eyes. "We're nowhere near the train tracks, so it couldn't have been a locomotive. What hit me?"

Before I could answer, a pudgy face loomed over us. Alarm and concern were written all over it.

"Are you alive, Sarah Jane? Can you get up off the ground? Can you see me?"

Sarah Jane closed her eyes again. "Wesley," she moaned. "How could anyone not see you? What I want to know is, why didn't you see me?"

"We were playing tag and Jason was chasing me. I looked back to see how close he was and when I turned around, there you were. You're lucky I didn't fall on top of you."

Sarah Jane shuddered. "Just think how close I came to saying farewell to this earth."

"Sarah Jane, please," Wesley pleaded, "can't you get up? Can I help you?"

Sarah Jane sat up like a shot. "Don't you put a hand on me, Wesley Patterson. You've done all the damage you need to do for one day."

Wesley backed off, and I helped Sarah Jane stand and brush off her clothes. By this time Miss Gibson had been alerted, and she hurried over to us.

"Are you all right, Sarah Jane?" she asked anxiously.

"Yes, ma'am. I don't think anything's broken."

"She just had the wind knocked out of her," Wesley offered.

Sarah Jane turned on him. "For your information, Wesley, my wind is what keeps me breathing. There's nothing 'just' about it!"

"Wesley, pick up her books and bring them in, please," Miss Gibson instructed him. "Come along, Sarah Jane. We'll go inside and sit for a while."

"You get my dinner pail, Mabel," Sarah Jane called. "Wesley would have it empty before he got to the schoolhouse with it."

"I really didn't mean to knock her down," Wesley said as we picked up her books.

"I know." I sighed. "But, Wesley, you're so big. You take up more space than the other two upper-grade boys together."

Wesley nodded miserably. "My pa says if I were a pig I'd be his prize moneymaker."

"Why don't you try not eating so much?" I suggested.

"I've thought of that, but my ma is such a good cook that I don't like to think on it for long."

Sarah Jane was still sputtering when I took her things to her. "He could have killed me. And since he didn't, Ma probably will. These are brand-new stockings." She stuck her leg out to show me a hole in the knee of one. "I'll be lucky if my skirt will cover the darning. Something has to be done about him."

"You can't keep him from eating unless you take his food away," I said. Sarah Jane looked brighter. "No," I protested. "I was only fooling. You can't do that."

"I don't know why not," she said. "In the interest of our safety and well-being, I think it's the logical thing to do."

"Miss Gibson would never allow it."

"I wasn't thinking of telling her," Sarah Jane replied. "This is a personal crusade. You and I can take care of it."

"Me? How did I get in on your personal crusade?"

"Are you my best friend, or aren't you?"

I had to admit that I was.

"Well, anyone who knocks me flat has knocked you flat also," she reasoned. "Share and share alike. Now, here's what we'll do: I'll ask to be excused to go for a drink, and on the way through the cloakroom, I'll take something out of Wesley's dinner bucket. Later on you do the same thing. If we do that every day until school is out, he may lose some weight. How does that sound?"

"Terrible," I said. "It might work today, but if he lost half his dinner every day, he'd howl. Then Miss Gibson would have to find out who was doing it."

"I suppose so," Sarah Jane conceded. "But today would be a start."

The others came in, and we couldn't discuss it any further. Wesley squeezed into the seat in front of us. Most of the students in the room shared desks, but in deference to his size, Wesley sat alone.

"He's going to get stuck in there one day," Sarah Jane whispered to me. "And when he gets up, the desk will too. We're doing him a favor."

Shortly after the opening exercises, Sarah Jane left to get a drink. When she returned, she took out her slate and wrote, "You won't believe it. He has three huge ham sandwiches in his dinner pail." She erased the *s* in *has* and put in a *d* in its place. "I took one out. You get another one."

About a half hour later I went out and stuffed a sandwich in my pocket. It wasn't long till I noticed everyone looking in our direction.

"What are they staring at?" I asked Sarah Jane.

"You smell like a ham sandwich," she giggled. "What did you bring it in here for?"

"Where was I supposed to put it?" I demanded.

"Girls," Miss Gibson interrupted. "Do you have a problem?"

"No, ma'am," I replied. "I'm sorry."

It seemed like a long time till dinner, and even I was beginning to get hungry just smelling Wesley's sandwich.

At dinnertime, we watched as Wesley ate his one sandwich, a piece of cake, and two apples.

"I'll say one thing for him," Sarah Jane commented. "He certainly is good-natured. He hasn't said a word about your taking his sandwich."

"Me!" I yelped. "What about you? You took one first."

"That's true," Sarah Jane agreed, "but it was the one in your pocket that he smelled all morning. There were plenty of places out there to hide it. Why did you bring it in?"

"Because I'm not as underhanded as you are," I replied bitterly. "Why do I always come out smelling like a ham sandwich while you come out smelling like a rose?"

"Good planning and organizational ability," Sarah Jane assured me. "We'll have to decide what we'll do next to help Wesley. Did you know he's wearing his pa's overalls because his own don't fit anymore? He really needs us, whether he knows it or not. That was a good idea you had to cut down on his food. Can you think of something else?"

I glared at her. "If I do think of something, you'll be the last to know."

"Don't be cross, Mabel," Sarah Jane said cheerfully. "I'll come to your rescue if you're ever hit by a steam engine."

"That's a safe promise," I grumbled. "You just take care of your own dirty work from now on."

Toward the middle of the afternoon, it began to turn quite warm. Miss Gibson opened the windows, but the soft spring day was more suited to dreaming than to studying. I was busy with my history when Sarah Jane poked me. She pointed at Wesley. He had given up all pretense of reading the book propped up in front of him and was peacefully sleeping with his head on his arms.

I watched in fascination as Sarah Jane quietly reached across her desk, unbuttoned the strap on Wesley's overalls, wrapped it around the post of his chair, and buttoned it back to his pants. Silently she indicated that I was to do the same thing with the other strap. I shook my head.

There was no way she could reach the strap on that side without standing up. Her eyes begged me to help her. Reluctantly I leaned forward and wound the strap around his chair. Blissfully unaware, Wesley slept on.

Sarah Jane's shoulders shook and her eyes watered with the effort to keep from laughing out loud. I turned my back to her; if she laughed, I knew I wouldn't be able to keep quiet. The scene we were imagining soon came to life.

"All right, class." Miss Gibson's voice broke the silence. "It's time for the history test for the upper grades."

Wesley sat up and rubbed his eyes.

"Wesley, will you please pull up the maps so everyone can see the questions on the board?"

Wesley started to get up, and then sat back down with a thump. Sarah Jane choked and clapped her hand over her mouth.

"Wesley?" Miss Gibson gave him a strange look. "Are you coming?"

"Yes, ma'am." He tried to stand up. "No, ma'am. I'm stuck."

Miss Gibson came back to investigate. By this time the room was rocking with laughter, and Sarah Jane was bent over double and gasping for breath. Miss Gibson's lips twitched as she freed Wesley from his chair, but the look on her face said that we hadn't heard the last of this. As for Wesley, his usually cheerful face was beet red, and he looked as though he might cry.

"I think we'll have the test on Monday," Miss Gibson announced. "It's such a beautiful afternoon, I'm going to let you go home early—except for Mabel and Sarah Jane. Will you girls stay for a few minutes, please?"

"We're in for it," Sarah Jane groaned.

Miss Gibson was very stern. "Do you realize what humiliation you caused Wesley?" she asked. "There is nothing more cruel than taking away someone's self-respect in front of his friends. I suppose you were also the ones who took part of his dinner?"

We nodded.

"Would you walk into the Pattersons' home and steal food from their table?"

I gasped. "Oh, no! We didn't steal it!"

"What else do you call it?" Miss Gibson asked. "I have never appreciated the teasing Wesley endures because of his weight, but this has gone beyond teasing. You have been mean to him. I think he deserves an apology."

"We like Wesley," Sarah Jane said miserably. "We just thought we'd help him lose a few pounds. I'm sorry we didn't think about how he'd feel."

"I am too," I said. "We'll go by there on the way home and ask him to forgive us. We'll never do that again. I promise."

"I'm sure you won't," Miss Gibson replied. She sighed as she looked at the hole in Sarah Jane's stocking. "This has been a hard day for all of us. But if you've learned something about consideration for others' feelings, maybe it's been worth it."

6

The Seamstress

"Ma, did you remember that we're having an ice-cream social at school in two weeks?"

"Yes," Ma replied. "I remember. And I'll have a cake ready for you to take; don't worry about it."

"It's not the cake I was thinking about," I told her. "It just came to me that a new dress would be nice."

Ma looked up from the bread she was kneading. "It would be fine, but I have more projects going now than I can finish in two weeks. Your good dress looks all right."

"How about letting me make it myself?" I ventured. "I'm sure I could do it. I've watched you sew all my life."

"I've watched Pa mend harnesses too, but I'm not going to try it," Ma retorted. "There's more to making a dress than sewing a seam. It's always nice if it fits when you're finished."

"I can't learn any younger," I said. "At least that's what you and Pa say when you want me to do something."

"You win, Mabel." Ma laughed. "I'll get the patterns out after dinner and see if I have something easy to start on."

As soon as the dishes were cleared away, Ma brought her pattern box to the table.

"Here, I like this," I said.

"I don't think you should try pleats," she protested. "You don't want anything with little tucks, either. They're awfully hard to make even."

"How about gathers? I could do that, couldn't I?"

Ma looked doubtful, but after going over all the patterns, she sighed. "That seems to be our only choice. I guess there's not a whole lot you could do wrong to a gathered skirt."

Sarah Jane was skeptical when I told her that I was making my dress for the ice-cream social.

"You don't have enough patience, Mabel. You know how you hate to take things out and do them over. You'll get tired of that the first day."

"What makes you think I'll have to take anything out?" I protested. "I could have it just right the first time, you know."

"I suppose you could," Sarah Jane conceded. "But you'll have to admit it isn't very likely."

She was right, of course. I had a habit of finishing things in a hurry and then finding mistakes. Ma was concerned about that too.

"Let me check each step before you go on to the next, Mabel," she said. "If you have to take something out, it will be easier before the whole dress is put together."

"No one has any confidence in me," I grumbled. "Why do you all assume I'll get things wrong?"

"We have nothing but past experience to go on," Ma replied. "But don't be discouraged. We learn by our mistakes."

"If I'd learned from every mistake I've made, I'd be twice as intelligent as I am."

Ma laughed and went back to her work. Later, when the dress was cut out, I began by putting the skirt together. Straight seams were not difficult, and when I showed them to Ma, she nodded.

"That's fine. Now pin the bodice together and baste it. We'll see if it needs tucks anywhere."

"Pin, baste, and sew," I muttered. "You don't do all that when you make a dress."

"Neither will you when you've put several hundred of them together," Ma replied. "Believe me, you'll save time in the long run."

The top of the dress was more complicated. After I had pinned the two sections of the back to the front, an extra long piece of material hung at the bottom.

"These parts don't match," I called to Ma. "You must have cut them wrong."

She came to look. "They aren't cut wrong. You didn't put the darts in the front."

I unpinned the pieces and placed the darts where they belonged.

"Aren't you glad you didn't just sew those together?" Ma asked me. "Pins are easier to remove than stitches." Ma was right, but I was in no mood to agree. I was already tired of the dress.

Finally I had the bodice basted together, and I put it on for Ma to check. But when I went to find her, she had gone out to work in the garden.

"I can't go out there in nothing but my underskirt and a dress top," I complained to myself. "And who knows how long before she'll be back."

I went back to Ma's bedroom to look in the mirror. The

dress certainly looked perfect to me. Why waste time when it was all ready to sew? Ma might be out there for another half hour. *I'll just go ahead and sew it up,* I decided, *and surprise her.*

Sarah Jane appeared at the door just as I finished the last seam.

"I thought I'd come and see how you're doing on your dress," she said. "Is it all done?"

"Don't be silly," I replied. "I've just started. But I do have the sides of the skirt sewed up, and I just finished putting the top together." I whipped it off the sewing machine and held it up for Sarah Jane to see. "Doesn't it look nice?"

There was a silence as she took the piece and stared at it oddly. "Hmm. But, Mabel, aren't you supposed to sew the seams on the wrong side of the material?"

I gasped and snatched it back. "What do you mean? Oh, no! I didn't turn it wrong side out before I basted it, and I sewed over the basting! What will I do now?"

"You know how much I hate to say 'I told you so,'" Sarah Jane snickered, "but my guess is that you'll take it out."

I rushed to the window and looked toward the garden where Ma still worked. "I can't get all those stitches picked

out before Ma comes in," I said. "She'll say more than 'I told you so'! I was supposed to let her look at it before I sewed."

"Don't stand there moaning," Sarah Jane said. "Start working on it. You'll never get it taken apart by having hysterics."

Suddenly I spotted Ma's scissors on the table. "I'll cut them off," I declared.

"You'll do what?"

"I'll cut the seams off. Then I can turn it wrong side out and start over. That way she'll never need to know."

"In all the years I've known you, you've never been able to keep anything from your ma," Sarah Jane told me. "You were just not meant to be deceitful. Or your ma wasn't meant to be deceived."

I was already cutting away the seams. "This isn't deceit," I replied. "This is survival. I'm learning how to turn my mistakes into intelligence. Put these scraps in the stove, will you?"

I turned the pieces wrong side out and was pinning them together when Ma came in.

"My goodness," she exclaimed. "Is this as far as you've gotten? Seems to me you were doing that when I went outside."

"I don't think I should hurry; do you, Ma?" I said. "I want it to look real nice."

Sarah Jane choked and hurried over to the water dipper.

"I guess I'd better go, Mabel. You've got a big job there, and I wouldn't want to disturb you." She rushed out the door, leaving Ma looking after her in surprise.

"She didn't stay very long, did she?"

"She stayed long enough," I told Ma. "And she'll be back. You can count on that."

I sat down with a sigh and prepared to baste the pieces together again. This time I'd let Ma see it before I stitched it on the machine.

"All right, Ma," I said finally. "Is it ready to sew?"

Ma looked critically at the front. "Something doesn't look right," she said with a frown. "Come here and let me see the back."

I went over to her and turned around.

"Why, what in the world!" she exclaimed. "It doesn't come together in the back! Did I cut it too small?" She took it off me and turned it wrong side out. "How wide did you make the seams?" She sat down and looked at it in bewilderment. "I can't believe I could have done that. And here I was talking about your mistakes."

Ma was so dismayed that I couldn't stand it. I threw my arms around her neck and cried.

"You didn't do it, Ma." I sobbed. "I did." And I told her what had happened. She put her head down on the table, and her shoulders shook with laughter.

"I don't see what's funny." I sniffed. "I can't wear a dress that doesn't meet in the back."

Ma wiped her eyes and picked up the bodice. "I suppose we could piece it," she suggested.

"Piece it!" I howled. "I won't appear at the ice-cream social in a dress that's pieced together like a quilt!"

Ma began to laugh again. "That's all the material I have like that, Mabel, or I'd cut out another bodice for you. Maybe I can salvage enough for an apron." She rolled up the skirt and top and handed them to me. "Put these in my room, please, and set the table for dinner."

I could hear her chuckling as she washed and cut up the vegetables. Somehow I felt worse than if she'd scolded me.

"I know what you mean," Sarah Jane said when I told her the story the next day. "If you get scolded, you know you deserved it. But if you get laughed at, you just feel stupid."

We walked a little way in silence. Then Sarah Jane began to giggle. "Your ma's not going to let you make the apron, is she?"

I glared at her.

"I was just going to suggest that if she did, the material would make nice carpet rags when you've finished with it." Sarah Jane ducked and ran up the lane ahead of me.

"You'd better run," I hollered, "or I'll make a carpet rag out of you!"

7

The Autograph

"Mabel, a package came in the mail for you today," Ma told me as I came in from school.

"For me? What is it? Who sent it?"

"How about opening it up to see?" Ma suggested.

Eagerly I tore open the wrappings and discovered a small leather-bound volume. As I picked it up, a letter dropped out.

Dear Mabel,

I have come into possession of a copy of John Greenleaf Whittier's poem "Snow-Bound." In remembrance of a similar occasion we shared, I would like you to have it. It is an autographed copy, since Mr. Whittier is a friend of my Quaker cousin, Eben White.

Yours truly,
Cousin Agatha

"Oh, Ma!" I cried. "Look at this! A book all my own! And signed by the author!"

"What a nice thing for Cousin Agatha to do," Ma said. "You must take good care of this."

"Oh, I will," I promised. "I can't wait to show it to Miss Gibson and the others. Maybe she'll read it to the school."

"Are you sure you should take it to school?" Ma asked doubtfully. "It's a pretty valuable gift."

"It will be safe," I assured her. "I won't let it out of my sight. I can't wait to see Warren's face when I show him. He thinks Whittier is the best author in our reader."

Sarah Jane was impressed when I showed the book to her.

"That's really nice," she said. "Your cousin Agatha must think a lot of you to send something like that."

I nodded. "I think a lot of her, too. After we really got to know each other, she turned out to be a nice old lady."

"But do you think it's safe to take it to school?" she asked.

"You and Ma are just alike!" I exclaimed. "Why wouldn't it be safe? Do you think I'll lose it between here and there?"

"It wouldn't be the first thing you'd lost between here and there." Sarah Jane snickered. "I couldn't begin to recall

all the stuff that has disappeared while you were looking the other way."

"Oh, for goodness' sake," I said. "This book is not going to disappear. Give me credit for some sense."

"I was just teasing, Mabel. I'm sure you'll take good care of it."

As I expected, Miss Gibson was delighted with the book. "This is something you will always treasure, Mabel," she said. "An autographed book is a special thing to have."

I had guessed that Warren would be envious of my good fortune, but I wasn't prepared for his reaction. He looked carefully through the book and studied the name written on the flyleaf.

"What will you take for this, Mabel?" he asked me.

"Take for it? What do you mean?"

"I want it," he said. "I'll give you whatever you ask."

For a moment I was speechless, but Sarah Jane wasn't. "You mean you'd pay Mabel for that book?" she asked.

Warren nodded. "As much as five dollars. That's all I have saved."

I gasped. "You would pay five dollars for this book?" That was more money than I had ever had in my life. "You can buy a copy in town for twenty-five cents!"

"Maybe so," Warren said. "But I couldn't buy the autograph. That's what makes it valuable."

I looked at my book with even greater appreciation and shook my head. "I can't sell it, Warren," I said. "It was a gift. I don't have very many books that aren't schoolbooks, either."

"You could afford to buy quite a few with what I'd give you," he replied. "But you think it over, and let me know if you change your mind."

"I'm sure I won't," I said to Sarah Jane as we left school together. "I can't imagine anything that I'd give up my book for."

"I'll say one thing for you, Mabel—you're not greedy," Sarah Jane observed. "Some people would sell their own brother to get five dollars."

"Don't think I haven't considered it," I said. "I just haven't had a whole lot of offers for Roy."

A few evenings later I found Pa sitting at the kitchen table, looking at a mail-order catalog.

"What are you looking for, Pa?" I asked. "Are you shopping for Christmas already?"

"Not exactly," Pa answered. "But I am thinking about winter. Your ma needs a new coat badly, and I'm trying to figure how we can get one for her after the crops are in. If we have a good yield, I might be able to afford this one." He pointed to a neat cloth coat that came in gray, navy blue, or black.

"Oh, but look, Pa. Here's one with a fur collar. Wouldn't that be warm and pretty?"

Pa looked at it wistfully. "Yes, it surely would. It would also cost about five dollars more than I can pay."

Five dollars! If I sold the book to Warren, we could get that coat for Ma. Excitedly I told Pa of the offer, but he shook his head.

"I can't let you do that, Mabel. Ma wouldn't hear of it if she knew. It's a very loving thought, though, and I thank you."

I said no more to Pa, but I thought about it a lot. Since the book was mine, I could sell it if I wanted to. And I did want Ma to have that lovely coat. Certainly after it was done and I had the money, Pa wouldn't object. I went to bed that Friday evening with the determination that I would tell Warren of my decision on Monday morning.

Before I blew out the candle in my room, I looked through the book again and studied the delicate writing in the front. What a beautiful name—John Greenleaf

Whittier. I sighed and put the book back. It was nice to have owned it for a little while, anyway.

On Saturday, as was our custom, Sarah Jane and I went to town. We spent the usual amount of time looking through the general store and surveying the new things that had come in during the week. I told Sarah of my plan.

"I guess you're doing the right thing," she agreed reluctantly. "Our folks give up a lot of things for us. Maybe we should try to pay them back more often."

We had just about finished browsing through the shelves and counters when Sarah Jane spied something.

"Mabel, look!" she cried. "Here's a copy of 'Snow-Bound' like yours. And it's just like you said—only twenty-five cents!"

I turned the book over in my hand. "It's just like Warren said too. It's not autographed."

"I don't think the one in your book would be too hard to copy," Sarah Jane said slowly. "I believe I could do it so you'd never know the difference."

"Sarah Jane! Are you serious?"

"Of course I am," she replied. "You'll have your book and the five dollars, and Warren will have his autographed copy of 'Snow-Bound.'"

"But that's forgery!" I cried. "It's against the law."

"Oh, for goodness' sake," Sarah Jane replied. "I'm not going to cash it at the bank. It certainly won't defraud Mr. Whittier. You can write whatever you want to in your own books. Are you going to buy it or not?"

I bought the book, and we hurried home with it. I had a nagging feeling that what we had planned was wrong, but I did want the money—and the book.

Sarah Jane practiced on a piece of paper until we both agreed that the signature looked just like the one Mr. Whittier had written. "Now I'm ready to put it on the fly-leaf," Sarah Jane decided. "Go sit on the bed or somewhere so you won't jab my arm. As nervous as you are, you'd probably tip the ink bottle over."

I sat across the room while she painstakingly copied *John Greenleaf Whittier* on the front page of the new book. When she had finished, she sat back and admired it.

"You'll have to keep these separated," she declared. "You'll never be able to tell which is the original."

I went to look, and I had to agree she was right. As far as I could tell, the signatures were identical.

"It's beautiful," I said, "but somehow I don't feel right about it. Warren will think he's paying for the real thing."

"He's paying for an autographed copy," Sarah Jane said. "That's what this is. If you have to be so fussy, show him both books and let him take his pick. If he chooses the wrong one, it wouldn't be your fault. You'd at least have a fifty-fifty chance of keeping yours."

I didn't chatter as I usually did while I helped Ma get supper, and she looked at me anxiously. "You're awfully quiet tonight, Mabel," she said. "Is something the matter?"

I shook my head. "No, I guess not. Ma, would it be wrong to sign someone else's name to something?"

"It depends on the reason for signing it," Ma replied. "If it was intended to deceive, then that's wrong. Under ordinary circumstances I'd say it's probably not a good idea. Are you planning on signing something?"

"Oh, no," I said. "I just wondered."

I didn't sleep well that night. I dreamed that I was caught in a snowstorm and Warren wouldn't help me because I had cheated him. I woke up to find my comforter on the floor and my heart pounding. Since I couldn't go back to sleep, I thought about going to church the next morning and trying to worship God. I knew I couldn't do it—not with the guilty feeling I had.

I soon discovered that I wasn't alone. Sarah Jane appeared right after breakfast.

"Mabel, you're right. We can't deceive Warren like that. I had terrible nightmares all night about what I did. I told the Lord I was sorry, and now I'm telling you. I feel bad about your money, but I don't think it's worth sinning for five dollars."

"It's not worth it for any amount," I told her. "I'd already decided that I would give Warren the real one. I don't want to remember any dirty tricks every time I look at Ma's beautiful coat!"

"Right!" Sarah Jane laughed. "And you said yourself that you couldn't tell the difference. I'll add my name down in the corner, and you'll have a real treasure to keep!"

8

The Farewell Party

"Mabel O'Dell! Are you absolutely positive?" Sarah Jane stopped in the middle of the road, shocked by my news.

"Yes." I nodded. "Absolutely. Pa told us just this morning. Miss Gibson won't be our teacher next year. It will be someone called Mrs. Porter. Pa's on the school board, so he knows."

"But we have only two more years," Sarah Jane wailed. "We've never had anyone but Miss Gibson. Couldn't she stay just two more years?"

"Pa says it's all arranged. I don't suppose we could talk her out of it, either."

"I think we'd better try," Sarah Jane declared. "How do we know we'll be able to stand this Mrs. Porter? She's probably old and crotchety."

"And doesn't like children," I added. "It will just ruin our ninth and tenth grades. What are we going to do about it?"

"We'll have to think of something," Sarah Jane said. "We may have to be such wonderful students she won't be able to leave us."

"Let's stay within reason," I retorted. "You're talking about eighteen human beings who haven't had much experience in being wonderful."

When we arrived at school, it was obvious that the news had already spread. Some of the younger children were crying, and I had to admit that I felt like it too. This was one occasion when all the children in school were agreed. We could not let Miss Gibson leave.

After the opening prayer, we joined halfheartedly in singing a hymn. Miss Gibson was perplexed. "What's the matter with everyone this morning?" she inquired. "You all look as though you'd lost your last friend."

To her amazement, the little ones began to cry again. "Why, whatever has happened?" Miss Gibson asked. "Is there something I don't know about?"

Warren Carter raised his hand. "No, ma'am, you know about it all right. But we just found out, and we don't like it."

"I don't understand," Miss Gibson said. "Just what do I know that you don't like?"

"Miss Gibson, is it true that someone called Mrs. Porter is going to be our teacher next year?" asked Walter Gibbs.

Miss Gibson looked astonished, and then became serious. "Yes, Walter. It's true."

"That's what we don't like! We don't want you to leave!"

"Why, I'm—I'm glad you feel that way," Miss Gibson said. "It's nice to be appreciated. And you know how much I love all of you."

"Then you won't let Mrs. Porter take over, will you?" Sarah Jane asked.

"I'm afraid that's all taken care of," Miss Gibson answered. "She has already been hired. But come," she added cheerfully, "we still have several weeks of school left to enjoy each other. Let's be happy and have a good time, shall we?"

Everyone settled down to work, but no one was happy—unless you counted Miss Gibson. Every once in a while we saw a smile on her face that disappeared when she caught us watching her.

"You're doing a lot of woolgathering," Ma said to me as I sat at the table that evening. "You haven't turned a page of that book in the last half hour."

"I know." I sighed. "I can't concentrate on medieval history when my mind is full of Miss Gibson leaving. I don't understand why she has to go!"

"You don't expect a young lady like Miss Gibson to spend the rest of her life teaching in the same school, do you? Maybe she has other plans that are important to her. After all, she's been here for eight years."

"I just don't like things to change, Ma. I want them to stay the way they are."

"Everything changes, Mabel," Ma told me. "We'd be in pretty sad shape if it didn't."

"I don't see why."

"If the good didn't change, the bad wouldn't either. I think God knew what He was doing to allow some of both in our lives."

"Maybe so," I muttered, "but I'm not very happy with the timing. Two more years is all I ask for. Is that too much?"

My question fell on an empty kitchen; Ma had left to get her mending.

"Are you still going to be teaching next year?" I asked Miss Gibson at recess the following day.

"Yes, I plan to be."

"Can you tell us where you'll be?" Sarah Jane asked.

"Not right now. But I'll let you know before school is out."

We didn't know much more than we had before. "I suppose we should plan a farewell for her," Sarah Jane said. "My heart's not in it, but we can't let her go without a party."

"Just remember to ask her to come," I said. "Remember when we forgot to invite her to her own birthday party?"

"We were just kids then," Sarah Jane said, dismissing the thought. "We wouldn't do anything stupid like that again. And, besides, you can't let past mistakes run your life. Let's go to my house and work on plans."

"All right," I said reluctantly. "But, Sarah Jane, isn't there anything we can do to make her change her mind?"

"This may be one of the inevitables of life," Sarah Jane said. "Miss Gibson has always told us that there are natural results of causes that you might as well not try to change."

"I think she was referring to natural laws, like gravity and death," I replied. "I don't think Miss Gibson is ready to fall or die."

We had reached the Clarks' porch, and as we opened

the door, Sarah Jane's mother jumped and pushed something under her apron.

"Goodness!" she said. "What are you doing here?"

"I live here, Ma," Sarah Jane answered. "Have you forgotten about me since morning?"

"Of course not, silly." Mrs. Clark laughed. "I just wasn't expecting you so early. Are you going to your room to do homework?"

"We have work to do all right," I answered. "We'll see you later."

Sarah Jane closed the bedroom door and sat down on the bed. "Did it look to you as though she hid something when we came in?"

"I thought so," I said.

"What could it be? It's not close to Christmas, and it's not near my birthday. What would she want to hide from her own daughter?"

"I'm sure you'll know when she wants you to," I told her. "Right now we have more important things to think about. When shall we have the party?"

"The last day of school," Sarah Jane suggested. "We can have all our folks bring food for a big picnic at noon."

"That's good. We should have one of the older boys make

a speech—but there is only one boy in the ninth and one in the tenth grade. Which will it be?"

"It's a sorry choice." Sarah Jane giggled. "Lester Blackburn is too shy to raise his voice, and Ted Simmons talks so fast you can't understand him. Why don't we ask your pa to do it? He's president of the school board."

"He might, I suppose," I said. "I'll talk to him about it. Shouldn't we give Miss Gibson a going-away gift?"

Sarah Jane nodded. "We don't have time to make anything, though. Do you suppose we could get enough money from all of us to buy something?"

"If everyone has as much as I have," I said with a sigh, "we could afford a couple of licorice sticks. Ma has a few crystal plates that she uses for wedding gifts; maybe she'll think this is just as important. I'll ask her."

I got home in time to set the table for supper, and I mentioned the plate to Ma.

"I think that would be nice," she said. "They're wrapped in a comforter in the chest at the foot of our bed. Lift them out carefully."

I located a plate and laid it on the bed while I put things back in order. As I turned to leave, I spied a scrap of lavender material on the floor.

"This is pretty, Ma," I said. "What is it for?"

Ma looked a little flustered. "It's about the right size for a quilt block," she replied. "I suppose that's what I'll use it for."

I had so many other things on my mind that I didn't ask where she had gotten it. I spent the evening planning a program for our party and making lists of all we had to do.

On the last day of school, I was both sad and excited. "You will come for the picnic, won't you, Pa?" I asked at breakfast.

"I wouldn't miss it. And I'll try to say something suitable for a farewell." His eyes twinkled, which should have warned me that there was a surprise in store.

At noon everyone gathered on the grass behind the schoolhouse. It was a large group, and for a time no one noticed the strange young man who stood near Miss Gibson. But we didn't have long to wonder who he was.

"Boys and girls, and parents," Miss Gibson said, "I want you to meet Mr. James Porter. He and I are going to be married on Sunday."

"Porter! Mrs. Porter! Why—you're not leaving at all; you're just changing your name!" Sarah Jane exclaimed.

Miss Gibson wasn't finished. "We want all of you to be present. And we're asking my four oldest students to stand up with us: Lester Blackburn, Ted Simmons, Sarah Jane Clark, and Mabel O'Dell."

There were a lot of congratulations and best wishes from everyone. The "farewell" party was a complete success.

"I won't sleep a wink between now and Sunday," Sarah Jane exclaimed. "I've never been so excited."

"What will I wear?" I asked Ma. "I don't have anything good enough for a wedding."

"How about that lavender quilt block?" Ma said. "Don't you think that would be nice?"

"You knew all the time!" I accused her. "And you let us worry about Miss Gibson leaving!"

"It didn't hurt you to worry a little," Mrs. Clark said. "But I was sure you two had seen Sarah Jane's dress the other day."

"So that's what you were hiding under your apron," Sarah Jane said. "I didn't think anyone could keep anything from us. I guess I was wrong."

"Don't worry," I told her. "You probably never will be again. But at least now you know how the rest of us mortals feel."

Sarah Jane made a face at me, and we ran off to congratulate our teacher.

9

Really Responsible

"Ma, why didn't you have two more daughters instead of sons?"

We were canning vegetables, and I was in charge of boiling the jars. Ma stirred the tomatoes before she answered. "I didn't have much choice about that," she told me. "I'm thankful to have one daughter. Sons are pretty nice to have too."

"I can't think what for," I retorted. "Why don't they have to stand over a hot stove once in a while?"

"For the same reason you don't spend the day in the field with Pa or milk the cows night and morning. It's called a division of labor."

"Not a very fair division if you ask me," I grumbled. "I'd rather be outdoors in the fresh air and sunshine."

"All right. I'll watch the jars and you go get some peas and lettuce from the garden," Ma offered. "It's time to start dinner."

"That's not what I had in mind."

"I know," Ma replied dryly. "What you had in mind was sitting on the fence, gazing out across the field. But that doesn't run a farm."

While I washed the lettuce at the pump and shelled the peas, I dreamed about what I might be doing in five years. My dreams definitely didn't include a farm.

"I think I'd like to go far, far away," I announced to Ma as I carried the pans into the kitchen.

"You've already been far, far away," she said. "You should be able to separate the pods from the peas better than this."

"I was thinking of my future," I told her.

"If your future is anything like your present, you're going to need a caretaker," Ma retorted. "I wish you'd learn to keep your mind on your work. Can't you see that it takes twice as long to do a job over again?"

Later Sarah Jane dropped in, and we sat on the porch to talk.

"I've been making plans for my future," I said. "There

aren't a whole lot of things a girl can do, but I'd like to do all of them."

"How many lives are you planning on living?" Sarah Jane answered. "I'd be glad to think of one thing I'd like to do."

I looked at her thoughtfully. "Your biggest talent is telling me when I'm wrong," I said. "There must be some way you could build that into a career."

I ducked as she swatted at me. "What are all these things you want to do?" she asked.

"I could teach school, or maybe be a nurse, or—"

"Or you could get married," Sarah Jane finished for me. "I think your best choice is right there. You could be a farmer's wife or minister's wife or storekeeper's wife or—"

"No, no," I interrupted her. "I've been somebody's daughter this far in my life, and I don't want to be somebody's wife the rest of it. I want to be successful on my own. I'd like to have a really responsible place in life."

Sarah Jane shook her head. "You're dreaming, Mabel. That would mean you'd be in charge of something. Can't you imagine what a disaster that would be?"

"Sarah Jane! I don't discourage you when you tell me about your dreams!"

"Of course not," she replied. "I don't want to try anything I'm not able to accomplish. What you have to do is suit your ambitions to your capabilities. When you get older, you'll thank me for my advice."

"Just don't stand on one foot until I do," I retorted.

But when I reported the conversation to Ma that evening, I admitted the truth of Sarah Jane's remarks. "That's the maddening thing about Sarah Jane—she's usually right."

"You've improved somewhat over the years," Ma told me. "But you have a ways to go. I appreciate every little bit of progress."

"I've never had any big responsibility to see if I could handle it, Ma. How does anyone know what I'd do?"

"Do you remember the parable of the talents that Jesus told? The master said that when the servant was faithful over a little, he would receive much. You have to prove yourself in small things, and then you'll be trusted with large ones."

"From now on, I'm going to be a responsible person," I declared. "I'll show everyone!"

"Responsible for what?" Roy asked as he came into the kitchen. "Seems to me you're already responsible for everything that goes wrong around here. What more do you want?"

"Now, Roy," Ma warned.

"I'll ignore that," I said.

A few days later, Ma asked me to sew some buttons on Pa's shirt.

"Sure," I replied. "Just as soon as I finish this chapter." I took the buttons and slipped them into my apron pocket. Before I had reached the end of the page, Sarah Jane arrived with some exciting news.

"How would you like to take a trip to Eastman with me?" she asked. "We're going to leave on the early-morning train and come back on the evening one. We'll have all day to look around town and have a picnic in the park. Won't that be fun?"

"I'd love to!" I exclaimed. "I think Ma would let me go. What day will it be?"

"Friday," Sarah Jane replied. "The day after tomorrow."

"That would be a nice trip," Ma said when we asked her. "It was kind of your folks to invite Mabel to share the day with you. Will you be taking the seven-thirty train?"

"Yes, ma'am," Sarah Jane replied. "And Mabel won't need to bring anything. Ma will have enough lunch for all of us."

"Perhaps you could pick up some yard goods and thread for me, Mabel," Ma said. "That is, if you aren't having such a good time you forget it."

"I told you I was going to be reliable," I said. "Of course I won't forget it."

Sarah Jane and I went outside to talk about the trip. "You shouldn't be promising things like being more reliable," she said. "You know how easy it is for you to have something on your mind and not remember stuff."

"If you weren't my best friend, I wouldn't have anything to do with you," I said. "Don't you think people can change for the better?"

"Certainly 'people' can," Sarah Jane replied. "It's just you that I don't have much hope for. But never mind, I'll help you remember what your ma wants."

I didn't have to be called from my room on Friday morning; I was up as soon as I heard Ma in the kitchen. My good dress and shoes were ready to put on, but I would wait until after breakfast to get dressed. As I set the table, I went over what Ma had asked for.

"You want six yards of a pretty blue print, eight yards of white shirting, and three spools of white thread. Is that right?"

"Yes," Ma said, "that's it. I'll surely be glad to have it. Pa and the boys need shirts in the worst way. Which reminds me—Pa is going to town this morning, and the only shirt he has to wear is the one you sewed buttons on the other day. Where did you put it?"

"I'll go see," I said hurriedly. "I think it's in my room." I knew it was in my room, hanging over my chair. But where were the buttons? I didn't have much time to find them and get them sewed on. I couldn't tell Ma that I'd forgotten about it. Frantically I tried to remember what I had been doing when she gave them to me.

"Mabel," Ma called. "You'd better hurry if you're going to eat. Here's Sarah Jane coming up the steps now." But I couldn't find the buttons anywhere.

I looked everywhere I thought the buttons could be and then went back and looked again. I could hear Ma and Sarah Jane talking in the kitchen, and I knew I couldn't stay in my room forever. Reluctantly I took the shirt and went out to face Ma.

"You've either done something you shouldn't or you haven't done something you should," Sarah Jane said with a sigh. "I can tell by the look on your face."

"I didn't sew the buttons on Pa's shirt, and now I don't know where they are," I blurted out.

"I'm not surprised," Ma replied. "I thought when I saw you put those buttons in your pocket that they'd be out of sight, out of mind."

"Oh! That's right! They're in my apron. But I won't have time to do what I was supposed to and still go. It's my fault; I can't blame anyone else." I looked imploringly at Ma. "Would you do it for me, just this once if I promise not to forget again?"

Ma looked sorry, but she shook her head. "I don't think I will, Mabel. I'm afraid there's no other way for you to learn than to repair your own mistakes."

I nodded and went back to my room to get the buttons. I couldn't help crying as I thought of the beautiful day Sarah Jane and I had planned. It was all spoiled, and it was my own fault.

When I returned to the kitchen, Sarah Jane was still sitting at the table. I wiped my eyes, sat down, and jabbed at a button.

"You'd better hurry up," I said to her. "There's no sense in both of us missing the trip."

"Shall I tell her before she finishes the job?" Sarah Jane asked Ma.

"Tell me what?"

"I just came by to let you know that we can't go this morning because Pa hurt his foot. We're going tomorrow instead. Now aren't you glad you have another opportunity to prove how reliable you can be? You won't get a second chance every time, you know."

"I'm sorry your pa hurt his foot, but I'm glad I can go. And who knows, Sarah Jane. I might live long enough to become as upright and virtuous as you are."

"Never mind," she said with a grin. "I'm willing to do anything I can to help you improve. After all, you are my best friend!"

10

The Tangled Web

"Mabel, it's time to get up," Ma called to me. Before I opened my eyes I knew what kind of day it was. Rain streamed down the window, and thunder rumbled across the fields.

Oh, not today! I thought. *How can we go to an outdoor birthday party in this weather?*

As I threw back the covers and sat up, the room seemed to spin around. My head felt light, and I was aware that my throat was scratchy. Well, Ma mustn't find out how I felt or she wouldn't let me go, even if the weather did clear.

But there was no way to keep Ma from knowing. As soon as I opened my mouth, it was obvious that I had a cold.

"Eat your breakfast," Ma said, "and I'll get a blanket and pillow for the couch. You can be out here today."

"Not all day," I croaked. "If the rain lets up, Mrs. Brooke may still have the birthday party for her niece."

"She'll have it without you," Ma answered. "You're not going anywhere in this shape. Anyway, it rained all night. I'm sure her yard will be much too wet for a party."

I knew Ma sympathized with me, and it wasn't her fault that I had a cold, but I felt cross anyway. "I'll be glad when I'm old enough to decide for myself when I'll stay in bed," I grumbled.

"So will I, Mabel." Ma sighed. "I don't enjoy this any more than you do. But until you are old enough, you'll have to go along with what I say. Now, would you like a book to read, or are you going to lie there and complain?"

I chose a book and read until my eyes closed. I didn't wake up till Pa and the boys came in for dinner. "It's clearing," Pa said. "That was a good rain. I think we can check fences this afternoon; the fields are too wet to work."

The sun came out. I was sitting in a warm place on the porch when Sarah Jane came by. "You look awful," she said.

"Thanks," I replied. "There's nothing like a visit from a friend to brighten one's day. I don't feel very good either, in case you're interested."

"I can tell you something that will make you feel better," Sarah Jane said. "Mrs. Brooke isn't having the birthday party today. She postponed it."

"Oh, how wonderful! I don't have to miss it after all! How long do I have to get rid of this cold?"

"Until Sunday."

I stared at Sarah Jane in disbelief and then glanced toward the door to see if Ma was in earshot. "Sunday? Mrs. Brooke is having her party on Sunday?"

"Yep."

"But we can't go on Sunday. Our folks would never allow it."

"I've been thinking about that," said Sarah Jane. "As far as I can see, the only way we'll be able to go is for them not to know about it."

"And just how do you plan to arrange that?" I asked. "My ma knows where I'm going, how long it takes to get there, and when I'll be back every day of my life. And yours does too. If that's as far as your plan goes, it's not far enough."

"I didn't think it would be. But you're good at devious plans. You come up with something."

"You're just full of compliments today, aren't you?"

"Don't be cross, Mabel. You want to go to this birthday party as much as I do. There has to be some way we can arrange it."

"Maybe we'd better work on your idea," I mused. "If our folks don't know where we're going, they can't forbid it." I thought a moment. "Did you tell your ma you were coming over this afternoon?"

"Didn't have to. She knows if you're not at our house, I'm at yours."

"That's the answer then. Ma will think I'm going to your place Sunday afternoon. Your ma will think you're coming here. We can meet halfway and go on to the party."

"Oh, Mabel! Do we dare?"

"Of course we dare. Who's going to know?"

Sarah Jane looked at me sharply. "Are you sure your conscience isn't going to kick you afterward until you tell someone what we did?"

"Consciences don't kick; they prick."

"Your conscience kicks," she corrected me. "You've never gotten by with anything in your life, 'cause if your folks don't find out, you tell 'em. Are you sure you won't do it this time?"

"Of course I'm sure! I'm not a child anymore, you know."

Sarah Jane got up to leave. "I'll see you later. I'd feel easier about this whole thing if I didn't know you so well."

By Sunday my cold was better, and I got ready to go to church with the family. It was a beautiful morning, and Ma quoted a Scripture verse as we got into the buggy: "This is the day that the Lord hath made, let us rejoice and be glad in it." My heart sank, and I was tempted to tell her what we were planning. But the thought of Sarah Jane's "I knew you would" kept me silent.

After dinner, I met Sarah Jane at the end of the lane, and we started toward Mrs. Brooke's house.

"I'm proud of you, Mabel," she said to me. "I was sure you'd back out."

"I'm not proud of me," I replied. "You know we're being deceitful."

"Oh, for goodness' sake, Mabel. You can't disobey your folks unless you do something they told you not to. We aren't doing that."

Her argument sounded logical, but deep down I knew better. I would go to the party because I'd said I would, but my heart wasn't in it.

"Come on," Sarah Jane said impatiently. "You look as if you were going to get castor oil instead of birthday cake. Can't you cheer up a little?"

"Don't you feel the least bit guilty?" I asked her.

"I probably would if I thought about it," she said with a shrug. "So I don't think about it."

I determined to stop thinking about it too and have a good time at the party. A number of people were there when we arrived, and the yard looked very festive. Mrs. Brooke had tied streamers in the trees, and a large table full of little sandwiches and cakes was set up in the shade.

Sarah Jane grabbed my arm. "Mabel, whatever you do, don't pour punch down your front or sit on someone's cake. If you get anything on that dress, your ma will know for sure where you've been."

"You sound like an old mother hen," I told her. "Why don't you just look out for your own dress?"

"I'm just trying to help you. I'm a naturally tidy person, but you're inclined to have an accident every chance you get."

I glared at her, but before I could reply, Mrs. Brooke saw us. "Oh, hello, girls. I'm so glad you could come. Have you been over to get refreshments?" She led us over to the table with an invitation to help ourselves.

We were so interested in the activity around us that we didn't notice when the sky turned black and a wind came up.

Mrs. Brooke called for everyone to go into the house, and the young men carried the table and chairs to the porch. No sooner had we taken shelter than the skies opened up and the rain came down in torrents.

"It's raining so hard that it shouldn't last long," Mr. Brooke predicted. But he was wrong. The storm showed no sign of letting up.

"We'll need a boat to get home in this," I said as Sarah Jane and I stood by the window and watched the storm. "We can't stay here much longer, or—" We looked at each other. We both had the same picture of her pa going to my house to get her and my pa going to her house to get me. When they found out we weren't at either place, there would definitely be trouble.

"Shall we make a run for it?" Sarah Jane asked.

"In our good shoes? If you think we'd be any better off by going home soaked to the bone, you're mistaken. They'd want to know why we didn't wait where we were until someone came for us."

Sarah Jane sighed and looked back out the window.

"Oh, what a tangled web we weave, when first we practice to deceive," she quoted.

"This is a fine time to think of that," I said. "If you're going to recite something, make it Scripture."

"Do you think God is angry at us for going to a party on a Sunday when we knew our folks wouldn't want us to?" Sarah Jane wondered.

"I don't think so," I replied. "The Bible says He causes the rain to fall on the just and the unjust alike, so it must not be a punishment. We brought this one on ourselves."

"You're probably right," Sarah Jane agreed. "And that means we have to take the consequences ourselves too."

Mrs. Brooke came over to where we were standing. "Is someone coming after you girls?" she asked.

"No, ma'am," I answered. "I don't think so."

"No one even knows where we are," Sarah Jane blurted.

"Oh, dear. You mean your folks don't know you're here?"

We nodded.

"We'll have to see that you get home," Mrs. Brooke said. "I'm sure the Carters will drop you off."

They were glad to, and we were soon on the way home. I was the first to be let out, and when I ran into the kitchen,

I saw at once that what we feared had happened. Mr. Clark was sitting at our table, and Pa was nowhere to be seen.

"Mabel!" Ma cried. "Where have you been? And where is Sarah Jane?"

"She's on her way home, Ma. The Carters brought us."

"What were you doing at the Carters'?" Mr. Clark asked me. "We thought Sarah Jane was here."

"We weren't exactly at the Carters'," I replied.

"And where exactly were you?" Ma wanted to know.

"We went to the birthday party at Mrs. Brooke's." I looked down at the floor, and the silence in the kitchen seemed to get louder. I wished Ma would say something.

Finally Mr. Clark cleared his throat. "Well, I'd better be getting on home. I'm glad you're back safely."

Ma saw him to the door. Then she turned and said, "You'd better get your clothes off, Mabel. They're damp."

"Aren't you going to punish me?"

"We'll talk about it when Pa gets back. Go along now."

Pa was drying himself off by the time I got back to the kitchen.

"I'm sorry, Pa. I know I did wrong."

"Do you know why we'd rather you didn't go to a party on a Sunday?" he asked me.

"Yes, it's the Lord's Day."

Pa nodded. "And we believe that Sunday is set apart for worship and rest. There are six other days to work and play."

"We didn't do anything but eat and talk. We didn't play games."

Pa put his arm around me. "You're getting old enough now to decide some things for yourself. How you spend your time is one of them. I hope you remember, though, that if you have to scheme to get something, you would probably be better off without it."

"Thanks, Pa. I'll remember," I said as I hugged him. Then I went off to bed, happier than I had been all day.

11

Gypsies!

"Whew! I don't think it's ever been this hot before!" Sarah Jane exclaimed.

"You say that every summer," I replied. "I try to think about something cool and not pay attention to the heat."

"It doesn't do you much good," Sarah Jane retorted. "Your face looks like a pickled beet."

We sat under the big tree at the end of our lane, facing the dry and dusty road. The heat seemed to rise from it in waves.

Suddenly an unusual contraption appeared around the curve. It looked like a house on wheels. The sides of the wagon bed were built up, and a canvas was stretched over the top for a roof. A dark-haired man walked beside the horse, and a woman with a shawl over her head sat in the doorway of the back of the wagon. Two little boys ran along behind.

We watched silently until the strange apparition disappeared from sight.

"Did you see that, Mabel?" Sarah Jane asked. I nodded. "Good," she said. "I thought maybe the heat was getting to me the way they say it does in the desert, when you start seeing things."

"A mirage," I said.

"A what?"

"A mirage. That's what you see in a desert. Only I don't think it looks like a wagon. Who do you suppose they are?"

"I don't know," Sarah Jane answered. "I've never seen them before. Do you imagine they live in that wagon?"

"There's not room enough in there to live," I replied. "Where would they cook and eat and do the washing?"

"It looked to me like they had all they owned on there. I saw cooking pots and clothes and everything."

"Maybe they're moving from one farm to another," I suggested.

"I don't think so," she disagreed. "There wasn't room for furniture in there. I think they live in it."

"Gypsies," Pa said when we told him what we had seen. "They're a group of wandering people. They stay awhile in one place, and then they move on."

"They'll steal you blind, too," Roy chimed in.

Pa looked at him sternly. "That's not fair to say. Not all Gypsies are thieves, just because an occasional one takes something. There are dishonest people in every walk of life."

Reuben returned from town with the announcement that the Gypsies were camped in the Gibbses' back pasture, next to the creek.

"Is it just one wagon?" Pa asked. "Usually they travel in caravans."

"Just one," Reuben replied. "It doesn't look like a very large family. I only saw two children."

"What do they do for a living?" I asked Pa. "How can they work if they don't live in one place very long?"

"Some of the men are silversmiths," Pa told me.

"And I've seen beautiful handwork the women do," Ma said. "I don't think I'd want to be on the go all the time, though. I feel more comfortable on a piece of land that belongs to me and in a house that stands still."

"I'd like it," I said. "Think of all the places you'd see."

"If you've seen one back road, you've seen them all," Roy said. "And besides, Gypsies aren't very well liked. You'd get pretty lonesome."

Sarah Jane agreed when I discussed it with her the next

morning. "You couldn't live in a wagon, Mabel. There wouldn't be room enough for all your stuff. You've still got the wood chips we used for dishes when we played house."

"They are memorabilia," I told her loftily. "I wouldn't take everything I owned with me. Just the necessities."

"You'd have to stop off here once a month to leave the memorabilia you'd collected along the road."

We talked about walking down to the Gibbses' to see if the Gypsies were still there but decided against it.

"It's not that we're afraid of them," I said to Ma as we did the dinner dishes. "But we didn't want them to think we were spying on them."

"That was sensible," Ma said. "I think they like to keep pretty much to themselves."

We were in for a surprise the next morning. When Ma opened the back door to call Pa and the boys to breakfast, she just missed hitting a little Gypsy boy who was standing on the porch. "Oh, mercy!" Ma exclaimed. "You startled me! Have you been here long?"

The boy shook his head and said, "Baby sick. You come?"

"Of course," Ma replied promptly. Quickly she turned, and as she buttered some biscuits and put ham on them, she instructed me to go ahead with breakfast. Before Pa got to the house, she was sailing down the lane with the little boy running to keep up with her.

"Do you think Ma should have gone over there by herself?" Reuben worried.

"Ma can take care of herself," Pa replied. "When someone is sick, you know she'll go."

"But Gypsies, Pa," Roy said. "They aren't—"

"Gypsies are people, Roy. They live differently, but they have the same needs everyone else has. God loves them as much as He does us. You know your ma doesn't ask people for their pedigree if they need help."

That closed the matter, but even Pa was surprised a little later to see the Gypsy wagon turning down our lane. I watched openmouthed as Ma jumped down from the back of the wagon and then reached up to take a shawl-wrapped bundle from the Gypsy woman.

"Mabel, fill the small tub with water, please. Put in just enough hot to take off the chill."

I scurried to do as Ma requested, and Pa went out to the wagon.

"This is Mr. Romani," Ma told him. "They were on the way to Canada when the baby took sick. Come, Mrs. Romani. We'll take care of her."

Ma soon had the baby unwrapped from the shawl and many layers of clothing. She sponged the feverish little body with tepid water. Mrs. Romani looked frightened, but she allowed Ma to do whatever she wanted to with the baby.

"I'll fix some warm water with sugar and just a drop of peppermint," Ma told her. "Then I think you should both lie down and get some sleep."

"I'd have a fever too if I had all that wrapped around me in this weather," I spoke to Ma after the Romanis had been settled in the spare room.

Ma nodded. "I know. They think babies should be wrapped up tightly to keep the evil spirits away. I don't think it's any more than summer colic, but she was so worried. It will be easier to look after them here than to run back and forth to the Gibbses' pasture."

The next couple of days were interesting to say the least. The Romanis did not want to come into the house to eat, so we ate outside. Pa set up one of the tables we used when threshers were here, and Ma made it plain that our guests were to eat with us. They listened quietly while Pa read the Bible and we prayed. We couldn't tell whether they understood or not, but Pa assured us that God's Word would not return to Him without accomplishing what it set out to do.

Mrs. Romani timidly offered to help, and Ma gave her tasks that she could do while she watched the baby. The little boys picked raspberries, and Pa reported that Mr. Romani was mending harnesses and sharpening tools in the barn.

"Are you going to ask the Romanis to go to church with us?" I asked Ma on Sunday morning.

Ma considered that for a moment. "No," she said finally. "I don't think they would be comfortable in an unfamiliar place. I don't know how they worship God, but they don't need curious people staring at them."

Pa told Mr. Romani that we would return shortly after noon, and we left for the service.

Ma had no sooner alighted from the buggy than she was surrounded by neighboring ladies.

"Maryanne, do you mean to say that you've had those Gypsies in your yard all week?"

"Weren't you afraid to go to sleep at night?"

"Could you understand what they said?"

"Did you leave them there alone while you came to church today?"

Ma answered each question pleasantly, but it was plain to see that she was not saying all she felt. I was glad when Pa returned from staking Nellie and we went into the church.

Ma's face was pretty grim as we turned toward home. "I declare, I don't understand people," she said. "Anyone should be willing to take in a needy family if they have the means. Why would we be afraid of a nice young couple like that?"

"Gypsies have a poor reputation," Pa replied. "No one wants to trust someone who has no roots and no hometown. People feel better about a person if they know his grandfather."

"Humph," Ma sniffed. "I've known some respectable people whose grandfathers were horse thieves."

We had only to turn into our lane to see that the Romanis' wagon was gone. The dire predictions of our neighbors were in our thoughts as we approached the house, but no one had the bad judgment to voice them to Ma. We didn't have to.

"I know what you're thinking," she said to us, "and you're wrong. The Romanis would not take anything from us. And even if they did, it doesn't change the fact that people are more important than things. They needed help, and we gave it. We'll do it again when the opportunity arises."

The house was quiet as we entered, and everything was in its accustomed place. It was as though there had never been a Gypsy family there. Ma took the pot roast from the oven, and I went to change my dress. The door of the spare room was open, and I glanced in as I walked by.

"Ma!" I called. "Come and see!"

Ma and Pa both joined me, and the boys were close behind.

"Why, did you ever?" Ma breathed.

On the bed lay three gold coins, two silver belt buckles, a bolt of cloth, and a beautiful white lace shawl.

"They needn't have done that," Ma said. "They might have used the money these things would bring."

"I think they figured they got more than money," Reuben said. "They knew you loved them, Ma. That's more important than things too, isn't it?"

"Yes, it is," Ma said, brushing tears from her eyes. "It certainly is."

12

The Expensive Bookcase

"Come on home with me, Mabel. I want you to see what I got for my birthday." Sarah Jane and I had been gathering berries in the woods and were on our way home.

"I hope it isn't a locket." I laughed. "Remember when you cut off my hair to put in your birthday locket?"

"Of course I do," she replied. "I still have it; though I need a longer chain before I can wear it. But I assure you that I'll never hang this birthday present around my neck!"

We went directly to Sarah Jane's bedroom. There in the corner stood a beautiful bookcase, painted to match the rest of her furniture.

"Ooh," I said. "Aren't you lucky? What are you going to put in it?"

"I had thought maybe books," she answered. "What else do you put in a bookcase?"

"You don't have that many books."

"I'm not dead yet. I might collect a few more volumes over the years. Besides, those shelves are nice for anything you want to display. I can put my doll there and some other things I've kept from my childhood."

"Oh, I'd love to have a bookcase like that," I said. "I have lots of things I could display."

"I'll say you have," Sarah Jane replied. "You'd need shelves from the floor to the ceiling on three walls to hold all you've saved. Do you ever throw anything away?"

"Of course I do," I responded indignantly. "I can't think right now what, but I'm sure I must."

"I'm not." Sarah Jane laughed. "Why don't you ask your pa to build you a bookcase? Reuben or Roy could paint it for you. It's not long until your birthday."

That night at the table, I brought up the subject. "Would you like to know what I want for my birthday?" I asked.

"We hadn't been worrying about it," Pa teased. "But if you'd care to tell us, we'll listen."

"I'd like a bookcase for my room. Sarah Jane's pa made one for her, and Josiah painted it. You'd be surprised how much neater I could keep my things if I had shelves."

"I think we might arrange that," Pa said.

"I'm in favor of anything that contributes to neatness," Ma put in. "That sounds like a fine present to me."

"I'll measure the space after supper," Pa decided, "and work on it whenever I can."

The bookcase was done by my birthday. It was painted a pale blue—my favorite color.

"Thank you, Pa," I said, hugging him. "It's the nicest thing I own. Doesn't it look pretty there?"

Pa agreed that it did. I spent the rest of the morning deciding what to put on the shelves. I didn't have many books either, but the ones I had went on the top. There were McGuffey Readers from the primer on up, a speller for each year, and several other schoolbooks. I also had two books I had won at school and the volume of "Snow-Bound." I added my Bible and was pleased with the results.

"Come and look," I called to Ma. "What do you think?"

"It looks very nice," she told me. "What are you going to put on the other shelves?"

"I think Emily can sit in one corner," I replied, "and Charlotte in the other."

As I placed the dolls on the shelf, Ma eyed Charlotte and shook her head. "Do you know how many years you've had that rag?" she asked me.

"Charlotte's not a rag!" I protested. "She's not as pretty as Emily, but you don't just throw away a doll that depends on you!"

"You have a heavy load of responsibility if everything you save depends on you." Ma laughed. "But this is your room. You keep whatever you like."

I arranged all the things I could find. The shelves weren't full by any means, but they looked very nice to me. I stood in the doorway and surveyed the rest of my room critically. The new bookcase certainly made my curtains look shabby.

"Ma, do you think we have a little material left from something that I could use to make new curtains for my room?"

Ma thought for a moment. "I'm not sure we have any scraps that are suitable or even big enough. Perhaps you could persuade Pa to let you go to town."

I was sure I could, so I enlisted Sarah Jane's help to pick out the fabric. "I'd like nice white curtains with ruffles and blue tiebacks to match the bookcase," I said. "Maybe dotted swiss."

"I hope you're going to let your ma make them for you," Sarah Jane said. "I don't know what you could do to a straight piece of cloth, but I'm sure you'd think of something."

"You're jealous," I retorted. "All you have is a new bookcase, and I'm getting a bookcase and curtains."

"I was just teasing." Sarah Jane smiled. "They'll look nice."

And they did. When Ma finished them, I washed the windows, and together we hung the new curtains.

"There. It looks perfect. Except …"

Ma paused at the door and looked back. "Except?"

"Well, the walls look a little drab, don't they? I mean, the windows are sparkling and the bookcase and curtains look so fresh and new. It does show up the old paint."

Ma sighed and went back to the kitchen. I wandered out to the barn to look for Pa.

"Would you happen to have any more of the paint you used for the bookcase?" I asked him.

"There's a little left, I guess," Pa replied. "What do you need it for?"

"Could I paint my bedroom walls?"

"Not enough for that, I'm afraid."

My face fell, and Pa looked sympathetic. "I could pick up another pail of it when I go to town. I'm not sure that you should paint it, though. Better let Reuben do it."

I stayed overnight with Sarah Jane while my room was being painted.

"What are you going to do next?" she asked me. "Won't your bedspread and rug look pretty old in that new room?"

"I suppose they will, but I haven't had them long enough to replace them. Maybe I could dye them to match the ribbons on the curtains. I wonder how much that would cost."

"Mabel! For goodness' sake! I didn't mean it. If you fix up that room any more, *you'll* look too plain to live in it!"

The idea stayed with me, though, and the paint was scarcely dry before I approached Ma about the bedspread and rug.

"That would be an enormous job," she told me. "They'd have to be boiled, and it would take the washtub to do it. It would have to be done outside, too. I'll not have my kitchen dyed bright blue." She looked at me. "On second thought, that's not a job you could manage at all. Those things would be much too heavy for you to lift when they were wet."

"I don't imagine you'd want to help me," I offered.

"You imagine right," Ma replied. "I don't have the time or the want-to. Your room looks lovely now the way it is."

I had to be content with that until I could find another solution. One afternoon an idea came to me. I was taking some cold lemonade to Pa and the boys, and I sat down under a tree with Roy.

"If I do something for you, will you do something for me?" I asked.

"What kind of something?" he answered suspiciously. "Who's going to get the short end of the stick?"

"No one," I said. "I'll do whatever you want me to if you'll dye my bedspread and rug. Ma won't let me try because the work will be too heavy."

"Anything I want you to, huh?" Roy thought about that. "It would be nice not to have to milk cows ..."

"I'll do it!" I said eagerly. "I'll milk for you."

"... for the rest of the summer," he finished.

"The rest of the summer!" I yelped. "That's another month! It won't take you that long to do what I want done."

"This isn't a matter of time spent, Mabel," Roy argued. "I'll be doing something you can't do. That should be worth a little more."

"I might have known a bargain with you would turn into a life sentence."

Roy got up to go back to work. "Take it or leave it," he said. "You're the one who brought it up."

I thought it over as I trudged back to the house. I could visualize how beautiful my room would look with just that one more thing done. But a month was a long time to face three cows morning and night. If I could get Reuben to take four cows while I milked two ... but Pa wouldn't allow that. Everyone did his or her share around our place.

After supper I told Roy that I would begin the next morning. Ma raised her eyebrows when she heard what I had promised, but she didn't forbid it.

"A month?" Pa said. "Isn't that a pretty long time?"

"She agreed to it," Roy said with a shrug. "If she wants a blue bedspread that much, who am I to complain?"

I sleepily followed Reuben to the barn before daylight. I had milked before, but only to help out, not as a regular job. Reuben was back at the house a good half hour before I finished.

"I can only carry one bucket at a time," I complained when I came in and found everyone ready for breakfast.

"That means three trips from the barn. You'll be ready for dinner before I get all this milk strained."

"I'll carry two in for you, Mabel," Pa offered. "I don't want you to miss your breakfast."

"You'd better start at least a half hour before Reuben does," Roy snickered.

Ma gave him a warning look, and he didn't make any more remarks. My new job didn't mean that I could slight any of my own chores. Long after Roy had fulfilled his end of the bargain, I continued to put in an extra three hours a day in the barn.

After a couple of weeks, I was heartily sick of our agreement. "I really like my bedspread and rug, Ma," I said to her, "but it seems to me I'm paying an awfully big price for them."

"I was sure you'd feel that way," Ma replied. "That has to be the most expensive bookcase ever built."

"Bookcase? I'm working for the bedspread."

"That's true," Ma said. "But think back. Because of the bookcase, you needed curtains. Then the walls had to be painted. Now the rug and spread have been dyed. That's often the way, Mabel. The more we have, the more we think we need."

Ma was right. "Isn't there something in the Bible about being content with what you have?" I asked her.

"Yes, Saint Paul said it: 'I have learned, in whatsoever state I am, therewith to be content.' That's not a bad thing to learn."

"I'm not likely to forget," I told her. "Every time I'm tempted to want more than I need, I'm going to see three cows looking at me. I'm going to be so content you'll think I'm one of them!"

13

Monday's Child

"Ma, on what day of the week was I born?"

"Monday," Ma replied. "You started the week out for us. Pa had to finish the washing that day."

"'Monday's child is fair of face,'" I quoted. "Do you think I'm fair of face?"

"That's a poem, not a promise," Ma said. "Beauty is as beauty does."

"Do you really think people's looks depend on what they do?" I asked.

Ma thought for a moment. "I think it means that your actions show what you are like inside. You can be a beautiful person even without having a pretty face. I've known people who spoiled their good looks by being selfish and inconsiderate."

"I guess that means you don't think I'm fair of face, so I'd better be good to make up for it."

Ma laughed. "You're beautiful to me, Mabel. And it certainly doesn't hurt to be good and fair of face."

When I saw Sarah Jane later that day, I asked her, "Would you rather be good or beautiful?"

"How could you make a choice like that?" she replied. "I'd like to be beautiful, but I don't want to be bad. On the other hand, I'd like to be good, but I don't want to be ugly. It's like asking if I'd rather keep my eyes or my ears. I need both."

"It was just a simple question." I sighed. "Why do I hear a lecture every time I ask you something?"

"Because there is usually something to be said on both sides of everything," Sarah Jane replied. "What did you ask me the question for?"

"I thought I wanted to know," I said. "What day of the week were you born on?"

"Friday. What's that got to do with being beautiful or good?"

"Miss Gibson gave me a poem to copy from one of her books. It says:

> *Monday's child is fair of face.*
> *Tuesday's child is full of grace.*

Wednesday's child is full of woe.
Thursday's child has far to go.
Friday's child is loving and giving.
Saturday's child must work for a living.
The child that's born on the Sabbath day is
bonnie and blithe and good always.

"I'd say that's a pretty fair description of Friday's child," Sarah Jane said, nodding. "What's your day?"

"Monday—fair of face."

"I suppose it can't be right every time," she said with a grin.

"That's what Ma thought too. She told me that beauty is as beauty does. Do you think that's true?"

"I don't know." Sarah Jane shrugged. "Why don't you try it and find out?"

"Try what?"

"Being good. See if it makes you beautiful."

"I am good!" I protested. "I don't think I'm a bad person."

"I'd agree with that." Sarah Jane eyed me carefully. "There are a few notable exceptions, but I'd say you come in with the best. But maybe some extra good deeds would help. What would you like to do for me?"

"Come over to study this evening and I'll help you with your arithmetic," I told her. "Will that be good enough?"

Sarah Jane nodded and turned toward home.

"You're the one who's loving and giving," I called after her. "What are you going to bring me?"

"My pleasant, amiable self," she called back.

Ma and I had almost finished the supper dishes when Sarah Jane came in and plopped her books on the table.

"You go ahead," I said to Ma. "I can finish here. Go sit with Pa on the porch."

"Well, thank you, Mabel," Ma said gratefully. "It will feel good to rest a bit. Be sure you cover the pitcher of milk in the pantry."

"I will."

I finished washing out the dish towels and hung them up. Then I stopped to look at the art project Sarah Jane was working on. We talked about it for several minutes when she reminded me about the milk.

I went to cover it. "Too late. There's a fly in it." I carried the pitcher to the table and set it down. "I'm not going to lose this whole pitcher of milk—come and help me."

"What are you going to do?" Sarah Jane asked.

"Why, strain it out, of course. Here, you hold the strainer over the sink."

Sarah Jane obeyed, and I quickly poured out the milk. She watched in fascination as the milk went down the sink and she was left with a very dead fly in the bottom of the strainer.

"Mabel, you are the only person in the world who could do a thing like that. Now what are you going to do with the fly, frame it?"

"I should have put a pan under it," I said lamely. "I just thought it was a shame to waste all that milk."

Sarah Jane shook her head. "Did you ever think of just skimming the fly off the top? Though I don't imagine your ma would want it anyway after it had a fly in it."

"That's what I get for trying to be helpful," I said. "I should have been a Wednesday's child."

"If that's an example of the good deeds you have planned, you can say good-bye to your beauty," Sarah Jane predicated.

"Oh, be quiet and sit down," I told her. "If you want help with your arithmetic, forget the smart remarks."

"I'm sorry, Mabel. It's just that the sight of that fly in the bottom of the strainer …"

"Sarah Jane!" I began, and then the ridiculous situation hit me, too, and I began to laugh. Sarah Jane joined in. We laughed so hard that Ma looked in to see what was going on.

"I don't remember arithmetic being that amusing," she said. "That is what you're doing, isn't it?"

We tried to concentrate on our lessons for the rest of the evening.

"Why is it that the good things I try to do most always turn out wrong?" I asked Ma later. "If I can't be good or fair of face, I might as well give up."

"I understand how you feel," Ma answered. "But just remember that when you have a choice between right and wrong, and with the Lord's help you choose to do right, you are becoming a beautiful person."

Ma's words were comforting, but I wasn't convinced that the best kind of beauty was on the inside. I wanted to be pretty on the outside, too.

On Saturday, Sarah Jane and I were looking through the general store, as we usually did. There was always the possibility that something new had come in since the last Saturday. Suddenly Sarah Jane clutched my arm.

"Look—over there by the door. Now there is a real Monday's child!"

I nodded in agreement. The girl who stood there was truly as beautiful as anyone we had ever seen. She had perfect features, and her smile seemed to light up the store.

"Did you ever see such long eyelashes?" Sarah Jane whispered. "And look at that wavy hair."

We were not the only ones admiring the young lady. Several young men were gathered around talking with her, and people walking by cast appreciative glances in her direction.

"I wouldn't ever ask for anything else if I could look like that." I sighed. "Just think how happy she must be."

At that moment an older woman approached the group by the door. "Come, Hannah," she said. "It's time to leave. Pa is waiting for us."

The smile disappeared from the girl's face, and she frowned at her mother. "I'm not ready yet. Pa can just wait."

"Now don't be difficult," her mother admonished. "You know we have to be home before dark."

The girl's look was stubborn, and she turned her back on the woman. "I'll come when I'm ready. You do nothing but nag at me. You don't care whether I have a good time or not." Her angry voice carried throughout the store, and Sarah Jane and I looked at each other in wonder.

"Why does her ma let her get away with that?" I wondered.

"Maybe because she's older," Sarah Jane suggested. "She must be seventeen or eighteen."

"I wouldn't answer my ma like that if I were a hundred and seventeen," I declared. "I don't think that girl is as pretty as she looks."

Suddenly Ma's words came back to me: "I've known people who spoiled their good looks by being selfish and inconsiderate."

"You know," I said to Sarah Jane, "Ma was right about beauty. If it's just on your face, you can ruin it with what you do."

"I'm glad you've realized that," Sarah Jane said. "Now you can stop worrying about how you look and concentrate on being a better person. There is always room for improvement, you know, and you seem to have more room than most people. Fortunately, I'll always be around to help when you need it.…"

I walked away and left Sarah Jane talking to herself; I'd heard it all before. It wasn't every girl who had two consciences to live with … but I wouldn't give up Sarah Jane for anything in the world.

14

The Fortune-Teller

"We have just two more years of school before we'll have to transfer to the town high school," Sarah Jane said as we walked past the empty schoolhouse. "I don't know whether I'm looking forward to it or not."

"I don't think I'll like being away from home all week," I replied. "I wish there was a high school closer than town."

"Maybe there will be in two years. That's a long time." She thought for a moment. "Wouldn't it be fun to know what was going to happen two years from now?"

"It might be," I answered. "But what if it turned out to be something bad? Would you want to know about that?"

"Sure! If I knew something bad would happen in two years, I'd do something to see that it didn't!"

"I don't know if it works that way," I said. "I know I have to help Ma with spring cleaning, and there's not one thing I can do about it. Except maybe leave home."

For once Sarah Jane didn't argue with my reasoning. It was plain to see that she was turning something over in her mind.

"I know one way we can find out what's going to happen in the future," she said at last. "There's a lady in town who looks at your hand and tells you how long you'll live, and if you're going on a journey or going to meet a stranger, and all sorts of other things."

"Sarah Jane," I exclaimed. "That's wicked! You know you shouldn't go to fortune-tellers! Anyway, how do you know about her?"

"My cousin Laura went with a friend to see her," Sarah Jane replied. "I don't think she's really a fortune-teller. She doesn't have a crystal ball or anything. Everyone has lines in their hands. This lady just tells you what your lines say."

"What did Laura's say?" I asked her. "Did the lady tell her something that really happened?"

"Well, one thing did, I guess. She said Laura would meet a dark-haired admirer on the street. Laura thought it would be a young man, but it was a horse! It ate the flowers off her hat. She figured it must have admired them."

"You're right." I laughed. "That lady's not much of a fortune-teller if that's the best she could do." I looked at my hand. "I wonder what my lines say. Do you know which one tells how long you'll live?"

"Nope," Sarah Jane replied. "But I hope it's the longest one. Why don't we go to see Madame Viola when we go to town Saturday?"

"Madame Viola?"

"That's her name. Or at least that's what she calls herself. Do you want to?"

"I suppose it wouldn't hurt to go just for fun. We don't have to believe everything she says. Are you sure all she does is look at your hand?" I asked.

"That's what Laura said. We won't have to say anything to our folks, because we always go look around town by ourselves anyway."

I nodded. Even though I really thought this wasn't the same as fortune-telling, something said that a discussion with Ma wouldn't be in our best interests.

"What if she told you that you were going to die at the age of twenty?" Sarah Jane wondered. "Do you suppose you would go ahead and die then because you thought you should?"

"I don't think anyone knows when we'll die except God," I said. "But I'll admit I might be a little uneasy around my twentieth birthday."

Later, as we did the dinner dishes, I decided to question Ma. "Do you wish you knew what was going to happen in the future?"

"I do know," Ma replied. "You're going to drop that plate if you don't watch what you're doing."

"I mean the future like five or ten years from now," I said.

"No, I don't," Ma said. "I have all I can do to take care of today without worrying about what's coming in ten years."

"I think I'd like to know if I'm going to be rich or famous. That would be nice to look forward to."

"'Seek ye first the kingdom of God, and His righteousness; and all these things shall be added unto you,'" Ma quoted. "God has promised us everything we need. I'm sure He would tell us what was going to happen ten years from now if He wanted us to know. Don't you think so?"

"I guess so," I said, nodding. "But you can't help being curious."

"Curiosity can lead to trouble," Ma warned. "You might find out something you'd rather not know."

I should have heeded Ma's warning and stayed away from Madame Viola, but I was as eager as Sarah Jane was to hear what she would say. We went straight to her little shop as soon as we got to town on Saturday. The sign in the window said: "Palms Read. The Future Revealed. 10 cents."

As we pushed open the door, a little bell tinkled and an ancient woman appeared from behind a curtain.

"Oh, young ladies," she greeted us. "Come in, come in. You wish to know what lies ahead, yes? Madame Viola can tell you."

Sarah Jane shoved me forward. "You go first," she whispered.

We all sat down at a table behind the curtain, and Madame Viola took my hand. With her long forefinger she traced the lines on my palm.

"Oh, yes," she murmured. "I see a long life for you, but not all will be happy. There is a move here also, and new friends."

A move? New friends? I didn't hear much more Madame Viola said after that. We had agreed that this was just for fun and we wouldn't believe what she told us. But what if she were right? I didn't want to move away or make new friends! I began to wish that we had never come. I didn't need to know as much as I thought I did.

The sun was bright and cheerful when we stepped outside of Madame Viola's dark little room. It didn't lift my spirits, though, and I scarcely heard Sarah Jane chattering about what she had been told.

"What's the matter with you, Mabel?" she asked. "Are you worried about not all your life being happy? Everyone has some trouble sometime."

I shook my head. "That doesn't bother me. I just don't want to go away from here."

"Is that all?" Sarah Jane scoffed. "You know she only says what she thinks she sees. She can't make it happen. I don't think you're going anyplace any more than I am." She sighed. "We wouldn't be that lucky."

Reluctantly I agreed with her and decided to put the whole thing out of my mind. "Let's go to the dry goods store and see if they have anything new," I suggested. We ran toward the store, and by dinnertime I had forgotten about Madame Viola and her predictions. I probably wouldn't have remembered them again if I hadn't been looking for our tabby's newborn kittens a few weeks later.

"I haven't seen them," Ma said when I asked her. "She usually hides her kittens pretty well until their eyes open. My guess would be the barn."

I searched around the lower floor without success. If they were in the barn, they had to be in the loft. I scrambled up the ladder just as Pa came through the door. He was talking to Ma.

"The only thing to do is sell," he said. "We can't keep it up any longer."

"I suppose you're right," Ma agreed. "I hate to let it go, though. We've had a lot of happy times in it."

"I know, but it's old, and we do need more room. Nothing lasts forever."

There was silence below me. I didn't mean to be eavesdropping, but it was too late now to let them know I was there. My heart sank as I remembered Madame Viola's words: "There is a move here also, and new friends."

"Do you have another one in mind?" Ma was asking.

"Yes, Wesley Blake told me of one for sale near his place. He said it would be just right for our family. I'll go see about it when I go to town Friday."

They left the barn, and I sat in the hay with my chin on my knees. The kittens were forgotten. Pa was going to sell our house and buy a bigger one! The Blakes lived at least ten miles on the other side of town. I'd have to go to another school. And I'd be without Sarah Jane. Even though she aggravated me sometimes by being so know-it-all, I couldn't imagine my life without her. We had been best friends since we were babies. I knew all her secrets, and she knew all mine. Whatever would I do?

I sat for a long time, thinking the situation over. I couldn't even talk to Ma about it unless I told her that I had overheard. I decided to go and share the news with Sarah Jane.

She gasped when I told her. "Mabel, are you sure?" I nodded miserably.

"I heard it with my own ears. And remember, Madame Viola saw it in my hand."

"I really didn't think those things came true," Sarah Jane moaned. "I'm never going back to see her again. Do you suppose your hand really does say that?"

We both looked at my palm and then compared it with Sarah Jane's. There was no difference that we could see. The lines appeared to be the same, and they didn't tell us anything at all.

"This has to be the worst day of my life," I declared. "Nothing this bad has ever happened before. We'll have to think of something."

"You'd better leave the thinking to me. You're liable to move yourself into the next state by mistake."

I was too upset to make a smart remark back. Besides, I had to get home to supper.

Ma didn't seem to notice that I wasn't saying much as I set the table. But when I pushed the food around on my plate without eating, she questioned me.

"Are you sick, Mabel?"

I shook my head.

"Then why aren't you eating?"

"I don't want to move!" I blurted. Everyone stared at me in astonishment.

"This time she's really gone over the edge," Roy declared. "I knew it would happen."

"Whatever are you talking about?" Pa asked.

"Madame Viola said I'd be moving, and I heard you say you were selling the house, and I don't want to go!"

"Maybe we'd better start at the beginning and sort this out," Ma suggested. "Just who is Madame Viola?"

With tears I told them the whole story, including what I had overheard in the barn.

"We won't say any more about Madame Viola," Pa said when I had finished. "I think you've learned your lesson about wasting your money on such as that. But as to selling the house, we wouldn't think of it. You heard us talking about selling the buggy and getting a bigger one." Pa's eyes twinkled. "Will that be suitable for you?"

Suddenly the heavy weight left my stomach and I was hungry. Everything was going to be all right again!

"I guess I don't want to know about the future," I told Ma after supper. "I'll just be glad to let the Lord send me whatever He wants me to have."

"I think that's wise," Ma agreed. "Very wise indeed."

15

Revenge

"Ma, do you know where my cameo pin is? It was in my room this morning, and now it's gone."

Ma shook her head. "I haven't seen it, Mabel. Are you sure you know where you left it?"

"I'm sure," I replied. "I was trying to fix the clasp when it was time to leave for school, and I didn't bother to put it back in the drawer. It was on top of the table."

Ma looked doubtful. "You've misplaced things before," she said. "I know you think you remember, but perhaps you don't."

"But I do!" I insisted. "If that Roy has taken my pin, he's going to be sorry!"

"Now, don't accuse your brother without any more evidence than that," Ma cautioned. "It could have fallen off the table, or you may have slid something on top of it."

I was sure that wasn't the case, but I went back to look again. A thorough search of the room revealed no cameo. When Roy came in for dinner, I lost no time approaching him on the subject.

Roy looked surprised; then he grinned. "If I did something like that, do you think I'd tell you about it?" he teased.

"You see, Ma? He doesn't deny it!"

Ma sighed. "He hasn't admitted it either," she replied. "Roy, I'll be glad when you're old enough not to torment your sister."

"He'll never live that long," I retorted. "He doesn't know how to do anything but torment me."

A few days later, my small comb with shiny stones in the top went missing.

"It's too bad I can't leave something on my own table in my own room without Roy meddling with it," I stormed. "Ma, can't you do something about him?"

Ma questioned Roy. "How come I get blamed for everything?" he asked. "I'm only one-fifth of the family. And not the most irresponsible fifth at that," he added, looking at me.

"I've never taken anything out of his room just to be mean," I said to Ma after he had left. "He's the one who thinks of tricks like that."

"I don't like these accusations, Mabel," Ma interrupted. "You have no proof that Roy has taken any of your things."

"But he never says he didn't," I wailed. "Nobody makes him own up to anything."

"We'll not discuss it further," Ma said firmly. "You put your things where they belong and they'll not disappear."

I felt the situation was grossly unfair, but I knew better than to say any more. Instead I glared at Roy when he came back in. If he didn't know what I was glaring about, he at least had the good sense not to ask.

About a week before Ma's birthday, Pa gave me a shiny new quarter to add to what I had saved for her gift.

"What are you going to get for her?" Sarah Jane asked me. "How much money do you have?"

"I'm going to open my bank this afternoon and see what I have. I'd like to get that new brush-and-comb set at the general store if I can afford it. Don't you think she'd like that?"

"I'm sure she would," Sarah Jane replied. "Will you get the silver or the tortoise shell?"

"They're both so pretty, I can't decide," I answered. "Let's look at them together on Saturday. You can tell me which you like best."

After school I went directly to my room and emptied my bank out on the table. One dollar and twenty-eight cents. With the quarter Pa had given me, there would be enough for Ma's present and three cents left over.

Just then Ma called from the kitchen. "I forgot to bring in the last of the eggs, Mabel. Would you please go out to the barn and get them?"

When I got back, I helped myself to the cookies she was taking from the oven.

"I guess one won't spoil your supper," she said. "Sit down and tell me how your history report went today."

It was soon time to set the table, eat supper, and help with the dishes. I didn't get back to my room until after family prayer.

As I scooped up my money to put it back in the bank, I saw at once that the quarter was gone. I started to call Ma and then realized that I couldn't tell her about the quarter. I'd have to take care of this myself.

"I'll get even with Roy if it's the last thing I do," I declared to Sarah Jane the next morning. "He'll be sorry he ever had me for a sister."

"I think that's already the case," Sarah Jane said. "But what makes you so sure Roy took all those things? I know he can be a pest, but he wouldn't steal."

"He wouldn't call it stealing. He'd call it hiding things someplace else just to make you look for them," I replied. "He needs a lesson he won't forget for a while."

"What are you going to do?"

"I don't know yet. You'll have to help me think of something."

"Me?" Sarah Jane exclaimed. "How did I get in on this?"

"You're my best friend. As you always say, 'What are best friends for?'"

The day passed slowly. I found myself reading a page several times before I knew what it said, because my mind wandered to the problem of what I could do to get back at Roy.

"Come and see the new kittens we have," I said to Sarah Jane on the way home. "Two calicos and a tabby." As we approached the barn, we could hear Roy sneezing. He met us at the door with tears running down his face.

"You sure got a nose full of something," Sarah Jane said. "What was it?"

"That patch of weeds beside the barn," Roy wheezed. "I forgot I was so allergic to them and waded right through it." He sneezed again. "I'll get over it if I stay away from there."

He went over to the pump to splash water on his face, and Sarah Jane pulled me into the barn. "There's your answer," she said.

"What's the question?"

"What you can do to get even with Roy," she explained. "If he spent a night sleeping on those weeds, he'd repent in a hurry."

"What are you thinking of?" I asked. "How could I get Roy to sleep in a weed patch?"

"Of course you couldn't, silly. I was thinking of bringing the weed patch to him. Stuff some of them in his pillowcase."

I stared at Sarah Jane in admiration. "Of course!" I exclaimed. "It would serve him right if he sneezed all night. I'll do it!"

At suppertime, Pa made an announcement. "I'm going over to the county seat tomorrow to file some papers. How would you all like to go with me?"

Ma's face brightened. "Why, how nice," she said. "We can take a picnic lunch and maybe even stop and see Harriet and Wesley Blake on the way home. We haven't had an outing like that for a long time."

Roy was excited. "That will be great, Pa. Do you think we'll have time to visit the horse barns at the fairgrounds?"

"I don't see why not," Pa replied. "We'll start early and make a whole day of it."

While we cleared away the dishes, Ma and I talked happily about what we would do the next day. "I think I'll get to bed early so I can get up and help you with the lunch," I said.

"That would be nice, Mabel," Ma said, hugging me. "I'm thankful for such a good daughter."

She might have changed her mind if she had known what her good daughter was up to. I brought in two large handfuls of weeds and pushed them into Roy's pillowcase.

Several times that night I awoke to hear Roy sneezing. Once, I heard Ma's voice as she spoke to him. *He had it coming,* I thought with satisfaction. *He'll learn to keep his hands off my things.*

Before daylight I heard Ma stirring, and I hurried to dress so that I could help her. We were putting things into the picnic basket when Roy came into the kitchen.

Ma gasped. "Oh, Roy! Whatever has happened to you?"

Poor Roy was hardly able to get his breath. His face was swollen, and his eyes were practically closed. Between wheezes he managed to tell Ma about the weeds.

"I guess I got more than I thought yesterday. I think they've poisoned me."

"Oh, dear," Ma said. "You're in no condition for a trip. I'll fix you some honeycomb and lemon and see if we can take care of it."

I was appalled. I had meant to teach Roy a lesson, not kill him. He would be furious when he found out what I had done. I decided not to tell him. I'd shake out his pillow and put a clean case on it. He didn't have to know I was to blame for his sorry state.

"I can't leave Roy alone like this," Ma said as we ate breakfast. "You and Mabel and Reuben go ahead and enjoy the day."

Needless to say, I didn't. The look on Roy's face as we drove off and the knowledge that Ma was missing the fun too canceled any joy I might have had on the trip.

"I suffered as much as Roy did," I told Sarah Jane the next day. "I guess that will teach me to believe what the Bible says about vengeance belonging to the Lord."

"Are you going to ask him to forgive you?" Sarah Jane wanted to know.

"Are you out of your mind? He'd clobber me!"

"You know what the Bible says about forgiveness," Sarah Jane said with a shrug. "I wouldn't want to live with that on my conscience."

"It should be on your conscience," I retorted. "It was your idea. I don't know why I always end up being the guilty party."

But in spite of my conscience, I didn't tell Roy what I had done. I pushed it to the back of my mind, and as the weeks went by, I forgot about it. One morning in the fall, Pa called Roy to the yard.

"There's a branch right over Mabel's window that needs cutting off," he said. "The first big wind could bring it down on the roof."

Roy got the ladder and the saw and prepared to do the job. A few minutes later, I heard him call.

"Mabel! Come here and see this!" He held out a large bird's nest. Inside lay my pin, my comb, and a shiny quarter.

"A magpie's nest," Roy said. "They're the worst thieves in the world—grab anything that shines. You must have had your window open."

"I did," I said, and I began to cry.

"Girls!" Roy said in disgust. "I thought you'd be glad to see this stuff. I'll put it back up there if you want me to."

Between sobs I managed to tell Roy what I had done and asked him to forgive me.

"I ought to smack you good," he told me. "But I guess you feel bad enough already."

"Do we have to tell Pa and Ma?" I asked.

"I don't," Roy replied. "It's up to you."

"Did they punish you?" Sarah Jane asked later, when I told her what had happened.

"Not in the regular way," I replied. "They felt so bad about it that it made me feel worse. I'm sure Pa's way of loving people instead of getting even with them is the best."

"I don't know why you can't remember that," Sarah Jane said with a sigh. "It would certainly save you a lot of heartache."

"*You* should be pounded," I told her. "I wonder if anyone else ever had a best friend like you."